For the Sake of Her Child
Kate Welsh

Love Inspired®

Published by Steeple Hill Books™

STEEPLE HILL BOOKS

Steeple
Hill™

ISBN 0-373-87039-6

FOR THE SAKE OF HER CHILD

And we know that all things work together for good to those who love God, to those called according to His purpose.

—*Romans* 8:28

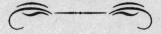

For those who believed: John, Heather, Kristen, Daddy, Mother, Debbie and my wonderful critique partners—Ardath, Bobbie and Martha. Your support has helped make a dream come true.

Prologue

"Why aren't the lights on?" Amanda Powers stared at her house from the drive, her stomach unaccountably jumpy. She rushed from the car to her front door. The unlocked front door did nothing to calm her disquiet.

"Keira?" she called, snapping on the hall light. Only silence greeted her. "Keira?" Silence. "Jesse?" she shouted, now irrationally calling for a baby too young to answer.

Dropping her coat and briefcase to the floor, Amanda rushed from room to room along the hall, turning on lights as she went. Empty. The rooms were empty. Could Jesse have taken ill? Had Keira taken him to the doctor—worse yet to the hospital? She dashed to the message board tacked to the refrigerator but there wasn't a note explaining the absence of Keira, her sitter, and Jesse.

She went back to her son's nursery but rather than finding evidence that Jesse was ill, Amanda was stunned to see that the diapers she'd left stacked on the shelf above the dressing table were gone. The closet was empty too, and all the drawers of the little chest she'd refinished just before his birth.

Like an automaton, she moved to the empty crib. And there she found the note. An innocent-looking eight-and-a-half-by-eleven sheet of paper told Amanda what her mind had refused to believe. What every parent fears and thankfully only a few ever face.

"I need a son. There was no other way. Keira."

Amanda walked to the kitchen and lifted the receiver on the wall phone. Surely, the world had stopped spinning.

"New Orleans dispatch," the voice at the end of the line drawled.

Amanda recognized Harry, her late husband Jess's partner. He'd been on dispatch duty since a shootout had left him paralyzed and Jess Powers dead. "It's Amanda," she whispered, her voice weak and shaking. "Keira—the sitter—she's taken my baby."

Chapter One

Garth Jorgensen checked his watch again. Five minutes past eight. One minute since he'd last checked, he thought, dragging a hand through his hair. "Where could she be?" he muttered and stood to pace the porch as he had been doing for over an hour. It wasn't long before he threw himself back into the swing that sat in the shadows of the wraparound porch. After a short time, he hiked up his sleeve and checked his annoyingly accurate watch. Even the happy, night sounds tortured him. How could the earth spin and all its creatures go right on chirping when his world had fallen apart?

A small car that had seen better days rattled into the drive just then, and Garth's heartbeat thundered in trepidation. The moment of truth with Amanda Powers had arrived. He wished he had an excuse to flee but he had no choice. This was what had to be done—what he had to do or never have a moment's peace again.

Garth stood as she approached her front door, his courage flagging. From his shadowy corner of the porch he watched her, unable to speak now that the confrontation had arrived. He wondered again what she was like.

Was her personality sunny?

Did she always look on the brighter side the way Jason did?

Did she still search, still hope?

He didn't doubt it. The copies of the newspaper articles the private detective had given him were heart wrenching and left no doubt as to the magnitude of the loss she'd suffered.

Because of him.

She bent and slid her key into the gleaming brass lock. The only feature Garth could make out was a fall of honey blond hair that swung forward over her shoulder, hiding her face.

Garth cleared his throat and stepped into the light. "Excuse me." To his dismay the words seemed to thunder across the space that separated them.

Amanda Powers gasped and backed away, holding her keys like a weapon. "What do you want?"

Garth winced at the tremor in her soft voice and the fear in her violet eyes. Stupid! How could he have been so stupid as to sneak up behind a woman at night?

"Sorry to startle you. I wasn't thinking. My name's Jorgensen. Garth Jorgensen." His words seemed to catch in his throat. "I—I'm, from Philadelphia. Pennsylvania." He paused, the rest of his well-rehearsed opening lines having fled his brain.

This was going to be even tougher than he'd imagined!

"Are you Amanda Powers?" he asked, trying a new approach. Garth patted the pockets of his bomber jacket. Finding what he sought, he stepped more fully into the light and reached out to pass the woman a copy of a seven-year-old newspaper article. It outlined the first six months of her desperate search. A search that had failed. "Are you *that* Amanda Powers?"

She didn't even glance at it. Her eyes stayed riveted on his face. She paled visibly in the harsh light of the carriage lamps that bracketed the polished wooden door. She took a hasty step backward and almost fell over a potted plant. The woman looked as if she might faint.

Amanda Powers dragged her gaze away from him and frowned as she tilted the page he'd given her to the light. Her hands began to shake.

"Jesse! Is this about Jesse? Do you know something about him? Please, tell me anything, anything at all that could help me find my son."

Garth's heart twisted to think of all the hours of anguish she must have suffered and all the joy he'd had over the past seven years. He swallowed. He couldn't put off the moment for another minute. "I think I've been raising your Jesse as my son. His name is Jason. That is," he added haltingly, "*I* have called him Jason."

Amanda felt her world spin and tilt. Could it be this incredibly simple? After all this time, when she'd exhausted nearly all her resources, could a man just show up on her porch to end her search? It could be another hoax, she warned herself. Don't get your hopes up! Why would he admit to kidnapping?

"That could be rather a dangerous claim, Mr. Jorgensen. Kidnapping is a federal offense. A death penalty offense."

"Yeah, I'm well aware of that. But believe it or not, I only recently learned that Jason isn't my son."

Amanda's spirits plummeted. "Then you must be wrong. My son was six months old when Keira Jagger disappeared with him. He wasn't switched in a nursery."

"Look, Mrs. Powers, this is a long, rough story. Could we go inside or maybe sit on the swing? It's been a bad few weeks for me and I'm just about played out."

Amanda stared at the man who claimed to have her son. It was uncanny how much he looked like her late husband, Jess. His eyes were the same brilliant blue and nearly the same shade of chestnut hair swept across his wide forehead. His cheekbones were high and his cheeks slightly hollow. His chin had the same little cleft that Jess had muttered about every morning while shaving.

Amanda wondered if this man's resemblance to her dead husband was the reason she felt a twinge of sadness for him—the man who claimed to have had her son all these years. There were lines of strain around his eyes and mouth, his brow furrowed as if he had one wingding of a headache. She waved him inside on instinct.

"Thanks, Mrs. Powers."

Amanda ushered him into the first room off the center hall. It was the only room in the house not crowded with packed boxes, except the one where Jesse had slept his first six months. That room had remained unchanged. She still hadn't gathered the courage to finally pack up the nursery. It felt too much like an admission that she'd never see her baby again.

She sat in the chair opposite the sofa and watched the tall good-looking man rake his fingers through his longish hair, then settle himself on the edge of the sofa.

"I guess I should start at the beginning," Garth Jorgensen said after a tense moment. "As much of the beginning as I've been able to piece together. A couple of months after your son disappeared, my wife, Karen, showed up after being gone for over a year. She had a child with her. She said he was my son. Please understand that I didn't doubt it for a second because he looked like pictures of me when I was his age. He still does."

"You and your wife were separated?"

Garth nodded. "Karen was...difficult. Things between us had been strained for some time. One day, she walked out of my life. I waited six months to hear from her, then I instituted divorce proceedings. Our marriage and anything I'd felt for her had been long dead."

He clasped and unclasped his hands. "But then she showed up with Jason. My mother had a baby picture of me on the piano for years. Jason was the image of me at that age. I had to take Karen back for his sake." He hesitated as if the next part were difficult to admit. "The truth is that I realized that Karen was...unstable. The problem was unmistakable within minutes of her arrival. I was afraid to trust her with the baby. I got her to agree to therapy but she kept getting worse. She killed herself by driving into a bridge abutment at nearly a hundred miles an hour before Jason was a year old.''

''She killed herself?''

''She tried to take Jason with her that day but my mother stopped her.''

They stared at each other for a long moment. ''Then the person who may have taken Jesse is dead,'' Amanda said at last. Curiously, she felt none of the victory she'd always imagined words such as those would bring. She felt only a hollow sadness. It was as Pastor Kendrick had always maintained. Vengeance was not man's province but the Lord's. ''Provided that the boy you call Jason is my son,'' Amanda added, afraid to pin too much hope on the word of a stranger.

''There really isn't much doubt. I hired a detective to find you when I first realized the truth.''

''Why did you suddenly find out that Jason wasn't your son after all this time? Why are you so sure Jason is my Jesse?''

''I had cause to go though Karen's things recently. I found a picture of you and your baby that was taken as you were leaving the hospital.'' He drew an envelope out of his inside pocket. ''On the back is written 'Amanda and Jesse come home.' It wasn't Karen's handwriting. I had it checked out. My investigator found you through it.''

Garth held out the envelope. Amanda reached out hesitantly. Her emotions warred.

Look at it.

No don't. He could be wrong. He could even be lying.

Why would he do that?

He could be another reporter. Don't do this to yourself. Don't believe him! You'll only be disappointed again.

Amanda closed her eyes and sent a desperate prayer winging toward heaven. It was certainly not her first prayer for Jesse's return but hopefully it would be her last. She gripped the envelope and ripped it open. And then she knew. Her prayers had finally been answered. Her search was over. Her baby found.

Tears of relief and gratitude filled her eyes. "Thank you. Thank you for coming forward. Take me to my son. Is he in New Orleans?"

"It's not that easy, Mrs. Powers."

Amanda forgot feelings of gratitude amidst her need to hold Jesse again. "Not that easy? Mr. Jorgensen you're in possession of a kidnapped child. I'm willing to give you the benefit of the doubt when you say you had nothing to do with his kidnapping but you had better not try to keep me from him."

"There are…complications. You have to understand, Jason knows nothing about you. He thinks I'm out of town on business. He has no idea about any of this."

"If you were this sure, why on earth didn't you prepare him?"

He dropped his gaze to the floor but not before she saw the utter devastation in his compelling eyes. Her scalp prickled as a cold sweat sent a shiver down her spine. The dinner she'd eaten at her desk turned to stone in her stomach. "What is it? Why didn't you talk to Jesse about this before you came here?"

"*Jason*. Get used to calling him Jason. He doesn't know who Jesse is."

"And whose fault is that?"

"Karen's," he said, honesty shining in his eyes, then he put his head in his hands. "Man, I wish I knew how she got so close to you, so close to Jason. I wish I knew how a kid could look so much like me and not be mine."

Amanda felt his pain and finally understood the confusion she'd seen in his eyes earlier. When he looked up at her, his blue eyes swam with tears he quickly blinked away. Amanda stood and pulled Jess's police photo out of a nearby box. "This was my husband, Mr. Jorgensen."

Garth Jorgensen stared at the photo then looked up at her again. "He could be my brother. He could almost be *me*." Jorgensen frowned, narrowing his eyes in deep thought. "The article about the kidnapping didn't mention when he died."

"My husband never lived to see his son. He was killed six months before Jesse was born." She mentioned the date in an automatic afterthought.

He muttered under his breath and handed the picture back. "Did the press mention that you were pregnant when your husband was killed?" Amanda nodded. "That's it then. Karen and I were in New Orleans that weekend, Mrs. Powers. I remember the date because the trip was a last-ditch effort to save a marriage that had nothing left to save. We'd had what I thought was a rational discussion Saturday afternoon and decided to separate. She was relaxing, reading the local paper when I went out on an errand. But she was gone when I came back. A note said she hated goodbyes.''

"But what does that have to do with her stealing my son?''

"I can only assume but she probably saw the article and the picture of your husband in the paper.''

Amanda could scarcely believe anyone could be that evil. "You think she saw got the idea to steal my son before he was even *born?* Could she have been that...that...?'' Any word other than *evil* failed her.

His eyes were bleak. "*Sick.* She was that sick.''

"Excuse me.'' Amanda stood and left, needing the refuge of Jesse's room. She walked to the crib and fluffed the little pillow—now yellowed with age. Trying to ignore its dusty smell, she hugged the teddy bear who'd guarded the empty crib for so many lonely years. Then she turned away. A sudden vision of the note as it had once lay atop that pillow flooded her mind.

I need a son. There was no other way.

Amanda walked to the other side of the room and sat in the rocker Jess had bought when she'd told him about the baby. She rocked, haunted by the thought that because of Jess's murder, she'd lost her son as well. Old anger swelled in her heart. Her husband had been so careless with his life in his search for acclaim—his search for earthly success. Now it seemed his death had even led to his son's kidnapping. She closed her eyes and prayed for peace and the ability to forgive Jess one final time.

Amanda looked up at the sound of footsteps. Peace

eluded her but strength filled her in its absence. "You asked how she got so close, Mr. Jorgensen. I'll explain after you tell me why Jesse still doesn't know that you aren't his father."

Garth nodded and looked around the little room. It contained so much less materially speaking than the nursery he'd furnished for Jason but he was sure every bit as much care had gone into its planning. How did he tell this woman that she'd found her child but could still lose him?

He looked around the room again and realized that Jason's room at home now held bunk beds and that teddy bears had given way to outer space. This room probably hadn't changed since Karen had taken the baby. Questions bombarded him. In Amanda's mind, hadn't her child grown at all in his absence? It made him wonder if that would be a normal reaction? He stared down at the empty crib. How strong had the ensuing years left Amanda Powers? Could she take hearing the rest of the truth?

Her wry voice called him from his troubled thoughts. "I'm not delusional, Mr. Jorgensen. My friends call it my shrine to Jesse but it's not. I just couldn't put his things away. It felt like a lack of trust in God. I've always tried to have faith that He'd bring my son back to me. And now that He has, I'd like that explanation you promised. Why am I supposed to be so all-fired patient before I see him?"

Garth turned back to her after sucking in a fortifying breath. Sitting in the tall rocker, she looked small and fragile and quite lovely. Her soft Southern accent wafted through the air as if her words had been spoken by an angel. He'd bet she'd never had trouble settling Jason for the night the way Karen had. A lullaby on the lips of Amanda Powers would surely soothe the most fretful child. But there was strength in her that belied her vulnerable appearance and she wanted the answer he dreaded giving.

"Jason's...ill."

"Ill? How ill?" she asked in a hushed whisper. It was as if she feared even stirring the air.

"He's in Children's Hospital in Philadelphia. This time it's just a secondary infection."

"This time?"

"There's no easy was to say this, Mrs. Powers. Jason has leukemia."

Amanda looked out the window of Garth Jorgensen's twin engine plane. He'd strapped her into the copilot's seat hours earlier. They'd stopped so he could top off his tanks at small local airports on the way to Philadelphia. Flying had never been one of Amanda's favorite modes of travel, but in Garth's small plane, it was more like a roller-coaster ride than air travel. It was a perfect metaphor for her life in the last few hours.

Amanda had always hated roller coasters.

She turned her head and listened as Garth spoke to the tower. He'd been cleared for landing. Amanda gripped the armrests even harder. She'd learned that there was only one thing worse than flying around in a toy plane and that was landing in one. She closed her eyes to pray as the ground came rushing up to meet them but the peace and assurance the Lord had always given her seemed to have deserted her.

An eternity later Amanda felt Garth's hand on

hers. "You can let go now. We've stopped."
Amanda focused on Garth, pleased for some inexplicable reason to see that an amused grin had lightened his care-worn features.

Amanda smiled, too. "It's not like riding in a 747, is it?"

His grin widened. "It's not like flying one, either."

"You pilot them, too?"

"Used to. I quit the airlines when Jason came along. That's when I started Liberty Express. That hangar," he said, pointing to a large building, "is our headquarters."

Amanda stared at the huge, freshly painted, cinder block structure. It had a Liberty Bell logo hanging over the large main doors. What sort of man had raised her son? His clothing didn't allude to wealth, but if he owned all this he had to be wealthy. Would he use that wealth to try to keep Jesse? "You own an airline?"

Garth didn't seem to hear the suspicion she knew was rife in her tone. "I'd dreamed about it for years. It's small but we're doing well. I had just added a cargo transport division to the commuter flights about the time Jason took sick."

"It sounds as if you changed your entire life because of him?"

Garth nodded. "He gave me a reason to chase the dream. I wanted something to pass on to him. I may go back to flying the big boys now."

Amanda had heard the pride in his voice when he'd pointed out the building that housed his company. Now he seemed not to care about it at all. "What about Liberty Express?"

"Whether Jason recovers and is able to grow up and live a normal life or not, I no longer have a child to pass Liberty on to. What's the use? Come on," he nearly growled. "Let's get to the hospital. We have a nine o'clock meeting with Jason's doctors."

"You've been flying all night. You haven't slept."

"Believe me, Mrs. Powers, I've missed more nights' sleep in the past year than I can count. And before Jason took sick, too. An airline pilot works long stretches at a time."

As he punched the correct floor on the elevator, Garth's stomach knotted. He was a mess, he thought ruefully. Not only hadn't he slept the night before, he hadn't slept in nearly forty-eight hours. He felt as if he'd eaten a handful of Mexican jumping beans. Glancing at Amanda, he realized that he wasn't the only one strung out.

"You're as nervous as a cat in a room full of rocking chairs. I promise, I've told you the truth about Jason's prognosis. And his doctors here at Children's Hospital are some of the best in the country."

"Then why couldn't I see Jesse first?" she asked as he directed her down a sterile-looking corridor.

Garth frowned. "Jason! His name is Jason. You can't slip."

"Why not? He has to be told who I am."

Garth sighed. She had longer to wait to claim her son. A lot longer. For him it was a reprieve—for her a sentence. He ushered her into the conference room. Someone else would have to explain why Jason couldn't be told her true relationship to him right away. He just couldn't do it!

Three doctors stood as they entered. Garth introduced Bill Wood, his lifelong friend and Jason's pediatrician; Matthew Hernandez, the oncologist, and Shelly White, Jason's psychiatrist. Doctor White took over the reins of the meeting immediately. "You must be Amanda," she said, holding out her hand.

Garth watched Amanda hesitantly take her seat, then listened to a recap of the last ten months of agony Jason had gone through. The first course of chemo. The first big disappointment when the blessed remission ended. Then the second course Jason had finished two months earlier. His heart ached when he saw Amanda's radiant face as she looked at the father-and-son picture taken of the two of them a couple of months before Dr. Hernandez had diagnosed the disease. He'd been such a beautiful child. But the ravages of the second full course of chemo showed in the next photo Shelly handed over.

The shock and pain on Amanda's face had him fighting tears once again. Garth felt that way every time Jason vomited as a result of the medicine they all hoped would save him. He felt again the panic and sorrow as he heard Jason crying and found him putting the hair he'd scraped off his pillow into a box. "I'm going to glue it to my baseball cap," he'd shouted, wiping furiously at his tear-stained face. "It's still my hair even if it's not on my head!" he'd told Garth in an uncharacteristic spurt of anger.

Garth had cried himself to sleep that night. Sometimes he felt so hopeless. What kind of God would let a child suffer like this?

"What are his chances?" he heard Amanda ask.

"We're not certain," Bill Wood replied after a quick glance at Garth. "Jason has been on the donor list for a bone marrow transplant for months but we're having trouble. So far none of the potential donors have been a good enough match."

"What about me?" Amanda asked.

Dr. Matt Hernandez shook his head "Doubtful. It's a question of what is called HLA Tissue Typing and it's much more specific than just blood type or parentage. You see, Jason got his genes from both you and your husband. In cases where there has been a lot of intermarriage, as in some ethnic groups or people from small villages, it would be more probable. In large American cities like New Orleans that doesn't usually happen."

"But Jess and I were from a small town. Nearly everybody was related in some way or another. Could that increase the chances?"

"It helps but it's still just a chance. And you have to be aware of the degree of discomfort—"

"This is my child we're talking about! I'd cut off my right arm to help him."

"That's what Garth said, too," Bill murmured. For the first time, Garth wondered if having his best friend—his champion—at this meeting was a good idea.

Amanda looked toward him for the first time since the meeting began. "Is that when you found out Mr. Jorgensen wasn't his father—when they tested him to be a donor?"

"Actually, we knew their blood types were all wrong from the beginning. We just didn't discuss that with Mr. Jorgensen at the time," Shelly replied.

"Why not? I might have found Jason sooner."

Bill Wood stood and stalked to the window then turned abruptly. "Because, Mrs. Powers, he was suffering enough already. Garth was devastated by Jason's illness and none of us thought it was necessary to tell him his dead wife had been cheating on him. That was the only logical reason we could surmise at the time."

Amanda blushed. She hadn't meant to be insensitive but it had all been so much of a shock. "Oh, Mr. Jorgensen, I'm so sorry."

"There's nothing you need to apologize for. No one's blaming you for any of this mess. You and Jason are the victims here," Garth said, shooting an angry glare at Dr. Wood.

"And you're not a victim?"

"Leave it, Bill!"

She studied Garth out of the corner of her eye. He'd been silent until then since entering the room. She looked down at the picture of him and her son. The illness that had decimated Jesse had done its work on Garth, too. She'd bet he had aged a year for every month since the photo was taken.

"How did you find out?" she asked, turning to Garth.

"While discussing Jason's condition with one of the specialists here, I learned that with my blood type I couldn't be Jason's father."

Amanda looked away from the pain in Garth's eyes. "What would be the procedure when you find a donor?'' she asked the oncologist, hoping to dispel the tense, thick silence.

"Now that Jason is in remission again, if we find a donor we'll use radiation and chemotherapy to ob-late all of the stem cells in Jason's body. We use transfusions to artificially elevate the red cells and hemoglobin. Then we do the transfer of bone marrow from the donor. The healthy bone marrow has what you could think of as a built-in homing mechanism that tells it where it belongs within Jason's body. Eventually it will grow into mature, cancer-free blood cells."

"What are the chances that it will work?"

"It's quite successful in cases like Jason's but it isn't risk free. The danger comes in the time just before and after the procedure. He'll be in isolation because he's open to any and all diseases. And be-cause his body's natural disease-fighting mechanism has been completely destroyed, he won't have the ability to fight anything off."

"Is there anything else? Why is he hospitalized now?"

Bill Wood took the question. "Jason cut himself on some broken glass. Just a minor cut, really, but because his resistance is low, the wound became in-fected and didn't respond to oral antibiotics. I ad-mitted him to watch him and administer intravenous antibiotics. It's a precaution."

Amanda nodded, calmer now, reassured that Garth had been truthful about Jason's condition. "When do you want to test me and when do I see my son?"

Shelly White cleared her throat. "As I explained, you can't simply tell him who you are. Emotional upset could affect his chances. He's in remission but stress could endanger it.''

"Then what do you propose I do?" Amanda asked, a hollow, sick feeling settling in her stomach.

"I think it would be best for you to be typed first. If you can be a donor then we can introduce you to him as such. If not, as a hospital volunteer."

Amanda propped her elbow on the table, leaned her forehead on the palm of her hand, letting her eyes drift closed. *I understand, Lord, I really do, but I want my Jesse back. Now! Tell me what to do.* The answer came to her and she knew it was the right one. She looked up at Dr. White. "I want to meet him now, as a volunteer. I can spend more time with him that way and if I can be the donor it will only bring us closer together."

"That's as good a plan as any. Garth, do you have any objections?"

Garth stood and shrugged. "Why ask me? I don't have a right to object." He grimaced. "In fact, I don't think I have any rights at all any more where Jase is concerned."

Dr. Wood scowled. "If not because of your love for him, then you have rights because a lot of the money for Jason's treatment has come out of your pocket and from the foundation your employees set up to help you with all the bills."

Garth gave the doctor a hard look. Always uncomfortable with the word *love* he stood. "I'm going up to visit Jason then I've got a flight."

Amanda watched Garth leave. He'd sounded so bitter. So sad. She hated that her good fortune had to hurt someone. His pain touched her deeply. Perhaps too deeply.

Minutes later, Amanda approached the room at the end of a third-floor hall with equal parts dread and anticipation. As she pushed her volunteer cart forward, the sounds and smells assaulted and soothed her by turns. Tears and laughter mixed, creating the bittersweet music of life and death—joy and pain. The smell of flowers and antiseptics warred, not quite defeating each other but blending into a smell that she knew would remain in her memory for all time.

Turning the last corner, she spotted Garth. He stood next to the doorway. His long straight back was pressed against a brightly painted mural of dinosaurs and vegetation. At his sides, his tightly clenched fists vibrated—in anger or pain Amanda couldn't tell. He stared straight ahead as if unaware of the sights and sounds around him, his expression blank.

Amanda drew up to him and stopped. She gasped at the pure anguish on his face. The sound drew Garth's attention at last.

"Is he awake?" Amanda asked.

"Awake?" Garth's attention seemed distant as the horizon they'd flown toward all night.

"Jes— I mean Jason. Is he napping or can I see him?"

Garth chuckled as if delighted despite his own pain. "He's poring over a book on New Orleans I picked up on my way to your place yesterday." His sudden grin faded quickly with a grimace of inner pain.

Amanda felt a pull so strong she had to force herself not to flee its danger. A moth to a flame, she reached out and gripped his arm, struck by the thought that, even as he traveled to arrange giving up the child he loved, Garth had remained a typical parent until the end. He hadn't come home without a present. "If he liked your gift, then what's wrong? Is he worse? What?"

"He..." Garth swallowed and wiped at a tear that leaked onto his hollow cheek. "He looks at me with such trust and I have to stand there and lie. I've always told him I'd be there for him no matter what and now it's a lie."

"You can be there for him as long as he needs you. As long as you need him. I want what's best for my son. If you're what he needs, then he should have you in his life."

Garth turned his head and looked at her with near desperation in his eyes. "I can't just walk away. I have to see this through with him. You see that, don't you?"

"Mr. Jorgensen, I just told you I did." Amanda put her head down and squeezed her temples, fighting off the ache slicing through her head. "This is all so unfair," she said in a broken whisper.

"Nobody ever said life was fair. I've got that load of freight to deliver and one to pick up in Scranton. When you go in, try not to act shocked because of how bad he looks. He's sensitive about it. His hair hasn't grown back in yet. And remember his name's *Jason.*

"I'm...ah...sorry you have to face this alone but I just can't be there when you meet him. I just can't lie to him again today."

Amanda smiled. "I'm not alone, Garth. Jesus is

always with me. He's kept me going for seven years. He won't desert me now.''

''You sound like my mother,'' Garth said, but instead of admiration for the faith she apparently shared with Garth's mother, there was bitterness tinged with ridicule in his tone. ''Where was your God the day Karen took your baby from you? And why did He let you find him when he's so sick a scraped knee put him in here?''

Garth turned and left as if he knew his question had no answer. None he wanted to hear, anyway. Amanda stared after him as her favorite scripture—the one that had kept her going for seven long years—floated into her thoughts. *All things work together for good to those who love God, to those called according to his purpose.* That would have been her answer but Garth clearly wasn't in any mood to listen. Seeing again the rigid set of his shoulders as he disappeared down the hall, Amanda wondered if he ever would be.

Chapter Two

Amanda stepped quickly out of the cab onto the sidewalk in front of Children's Hospital, then rushed toward the entrance, anxious to meet Jesse. No, Jason! She had to remember that or she was going to endanger his health. And he did look so weak. He'd been asleep the day before and Amanda, after watching him sleep for a couple of hours, had left at a nurse's urging.

Amanda had resented the intrusion but understood when she'd seen herself in a mirror. It hadn't been a pretty sight. The dingy mirror in her motel room that morning showed the improvement sleep, a shower and fresh makeup could make. Amanda smiled. What was it her grandmother used to say about women and makeup? "Even an old barn looks better with a fresh coat of paint." It certainly held true for her today.

After picking up her volunteer cart, Amanda rushed to Jason's room. A high-pitched giggle and the sound of a deep voice froze her in her tracks.

"Well, thanks for the high praise, son. I'll have to come up with as nice a compliment to give you now."

"How about my head has a healthy shine today?" a laughing child asked.

"Oh, I don't know. I swear I see a little peach fuzz dulling that chrome dome," a voice she recognized as Garth's responded.

Garth's unkind comment hit Amanda like a physical slap, but what shocked her more was the child's giggle that followed in response. Then a thick silence descended.

"It'll grow back, won't it, Daddy?" All the glee had left the boy's tone. "And I really will be healthy again?"

"Hey! Of course you will. You'll be totally healthy—and hairy," he quipped in a lighthearted voice, "in no time. I promised you, didn't I? Have I ever broken a promise?" There was a long pause. "Well, there you have it. A Garth Jorgensen promise is as good as gold. Why, I'll bet you we find a donor any day. That'll really cinch it."

Amanda braced her back against the door and pushed inward. She couldn't wait longer. "Hello there. My name's Amanda Powers. I'm the new volunteer on this wing," she announced, hoping she sounded more cheerful and matter-of-fact than she felt. She backed her book and toy laden cart into the room then turned, hoping she was once again mentally braced and ready for the sight of her dangerously ill son.

She wasn't ready. Not by a long shot! Her plump, healthy baby was now unrecognizable in this thin, tired boy in the hospital bed. How could Garth manage to joke about Jason's appearance?

"Hi. I'm Jason Jorgensen. This is Garth Jorgensen. He's my dad. We don't look much alike right now but we used to. After I saw *The King and I,* I decided I was the king in a former life."

"You believe in reincarnation?" Amanda asked, fascinated by so adult a statement from so young a child but worried about what he'd been taught.

"Nah. I was just joking," he waved away the notion with an arm attached to an IV tube that connected to the bag hanging over his head. Amanda stared in fascinated horror at Jason's hand where the needle penetrated. "I like what my dad told me better."

Amanda glanced at Garth who remained silent, his face a noncommittal mask. "What did he teach you?"

"That 'cause I'm a kid, if I die I go right to heaven and being there puts this life to shame. He says there's a room in a palace just waiting for me. And Dad says that if I get too tired of fighting, the angels will take me there. But if I want to get better, then he'll help me keep fighting."

"I—I see. We'll all help you fight, Jason," she said, surprised that Garth would handle the subject the way he had. How had he found the strength inside himself to tell the child he held dear that he was free to leave life behind if he needed to? Especially since he seemed to rail against God because of the illness that might take Jason.

"I won't give up though," Jason promised staring at Garth. "Dad says I'm a fighter. Right, Dad?"

Garth nodded, still silent. Amanda watched a poignant exchange between father and son. Garth stood and looked at his watch. "I've got to be going, kiddo. I'll bring you that treat if you promise not to give the nurse a hard time about today's blood tests."

"Ah, don't worry about me. I bet these are the best marks yet. I studied hard for 'em this time!"

Garth chuckled as Amanda wondered at the strange combination her son seemed to be. She'd just had a rational, very adult conversation about death with him and yet he had the wonderful faith in God that few other than children seemed able to hold on to. Seconds later he'd gladly accepted bribery from Garth for his good behavior then wisecracked like a boy three times his age. He seemed and—considering his bald head and thin face—looked like a little old man with the body and voice of a child.

Garth leaned down and kissed the boy, tugged on the teenager's cap, and allowed the old man in Jason to draw strength from their embrace.

"Nice meeting you, Mrs. Powers," Garth said. "Have a nice visit but don't let him chew your ear off."

Amanda watched Garth leave then turned to Jason. They were father and son, as much as she hated to admit it. She, the one with all the legal rights, was on the outside looking in. It might not be right or fair but that was how it was.

"Sure hope these tests are good," Jason muttered, shaking his head. Again, he'd aged.

"You seem to want it for more than just that it means you're getting better. Why?"

"My dad needs me and I'm getting awful tired of

fighting. I'm his reason for living. He told me that once. It was before I got sick. It wouldn't be fair not to fight till I can't anymore. It isn't just me, you see?"

"Yes," Amanda said, choking on tears she dared not show. "Yes, I see. You love your father very much."

Jason nodded. "My dad's a real live hero."

"Hero?" Amanda frowned. They'd called Jess, his real father, a hero, too. Wanting it—the accolades, the admiration—had killed him. Why thoughts of Garth traveling the same dangerous path bothered her, Amanda couldn't say. She only knew that inexplicably it did.

"...but Dad stayed in the Air Force Reserve," her son was saying. "He was in Desert Storm and he saved a whole lot of people. I was there when he got his medal and a general talked about how my dad risked his life to save soldiers he didn't even know. Dad quit though when I got sick. Grandmom lives with us and my aunt Christina only lives two miles away from our house. They take care of me when he's working and when he used to go away. I sure miss my aunt Chris. I prayed she'd come see me today."

A tap on the door drew Amanda's attention. "Aunt Chris! Guess what! Jesus answered my prayer. I wanted you to come today and here you are. Just like you said. He really answers some prayers quick."

"Just don't forget the other part," the tall blonde in the doorway said.

"I know. He's telling me to wait when I pray about my leukemia. Come meet my new friend."

As the door pushed fully open, the young woman walked in with a balloon and a gift. Her classic features and bright blue eyes marked her as Garth's sister at once, even though she had light hair instead of Garth's rich chestnut.

"So, what's this I hear about my klutzy favorite nephew and a broken bottle? Honestly, I go on a business trip and you wind up in here. What are we going to do with you?"

Jason shrugged. A gesture so like one she'd seen Garth make that it made Amanda's heart ache. "Give me my present?" he asked hopefully.

Garth's sister handed over the gift and turned to Amanda with a smile. "Hello. I guess you're new around here."

"This is Mrs. Powers. Her first name's Amanda," Jason said as he tore into the package. "She's the new volunteer. I was just telling her about what a big hero Dad is."

Christina's smile faded. "Mrs. Powers. I...I'm pleased to meet you."

"It's good to meet you, too," Amanda said, realizing Christina knew who she was and that the meeting was not a pleasure for the other woman at all. She cast about for something to say that would ease the awkward situation. "Jason was just telling me that your brother is in the Air Force Reserve."

"*Was*. He resigned his commission about a year ago."

"When I got sick," Jason said, his tone suddenly

sullen. "I wrecked everything by getting sick. He'd be a major by now if it wasn't for me!"

"Jason Jorgensen! What a thing to say. Your father loves you. He didn't give a fig about his rank and you know it. He quit to spend more time with you."

Jason sank back on his pillow after a careless shrug that was anything but careless. He clearly felt he'd become a burden on Garth. "'Cause I might not be here for long."

Christina whispered, "Get his shrink," as she passed Amanda to sit on the bed next to Jason. "Is it time for a pity party?" she asked gently as she settled next to her nephew.

Amanda didn't wait for his answer. She pushed her cart into the hall and went to the nurses' station to call Dr. Shelly White.

What had happened to the happy little boy Garth had left in her care? She knew it was foolish but she felt as if she had somehow failed her son already.

Garth entered the hospital just after dark. His stomach hurt from lack of food but hunger would have to wait. Most nights he stayed far past regular visiting hours, helping get Jason settled for sleep. Often he even stayed until his son dropped off.

His son? Not for long. No, that wasn't true. Legally he didn't have a single right to call Jason son but in his heart that boy would be his son into eternity. Garth stabbed the button, calling the elevator. How could Karen have done this?

"You gettin' on the elevator or what, mister?" an impatient voice snapped from behind.

Garth looked up startled to see an open elevator before him. He stepped in, apologizing to the elderly man whose path he'd inadvertently blocked. Minutes later, he stepped into Jason's room, surprised to find Amanda embroiled in a Monopoly game with the only eight-year-old business tycoon he'd ever met. He smiled when he saw the healthy stacks of colorful money tucked under Jason's side of the board. Jason appeared to be over the setback Chris had called his office about and Amanda looked about ready for the poorhouse. It didn't take a genius to figure out who owned all those little red hotels lined up around the board.

"You could lend me the hundred and fifty," Amanda was saying as he let the door drift closed. "I'll be past Go by my next turn."

Jason wiggled his eyebrows. "Or you could sell me..." He paused and tapped his chin. "Let's see...how about your Electric Company."

"*My last utility?* You little rat! You've been after those since I bought the first one."

Jason snickered. "And now I've got all but one! Come on, Mrs. Powers, pay the rent." Snidely Whiplash had nothing on his son, Garth decided wryly.

"But I can't pay the rent," Amanda sighed dramatically, picking up on the joke.

"But you must pay the rent," Jason ordered in an unnaturally deep voice.

"I'll pay the rent!" Garth shouted, then strode forward and plopped down a paper bag in the middle of the game board.

The game forgotten, Jason scooped up the bag and tore it open. "Wow! Are these all for me?"

Garth raised an eyebrow. "You have a guest, kiddo."

"Oh! Sorry, Mrs. Powers. Would you like one? They're my Grandmom's cookies. She's the best baker in the whole world." Garth's heart contracted painfully when he saw the nearly worshipful look in his son's eyes when he looked at her.

"I guess I'd better not pass up the world's number one cook's cookies," Amanda replied, her boundless love easily readable in her eyes.

Garth wondered what it would be like to have Amanda Powers look at him like that. He pushed the thought away. He was no good at relationships. And even if he were, getting more involved in Amanda's life was out of the question. It could only lead to more heartache than he could stand.

His son obviously had other ideas. "No, she's a lousy cook. She's just a great *baker*. Mrs. Powers hasn't eaten, Dad," Jason hinted. "And I know you haven't."

"Then she shouldn't have another cookie. It'll spoil her appetite."

Jason pressed on. "Dad does anything to avoid Grandmom's cooking. He comes straight here and eats on his way home. He uses me as an excuse. Why don't you take Mrs. Powers to dinner? She ate breakfast and lunch here and she's got to be starving. She'll think Philly has awful food."

"I'm sure Mrs. Powers knows hospital food doesn't represent the best Philadelphia has to offer. I'm also sure she doesn't need me to prove it to her." Garth didn't glance at Amanda but that was probably a mistake because it left him looking into his son's disappointed eyes. The kid had had a rough day with all the tests and whatever had upset him while Chris had been there. Garth decided it wouldn't hurt him to take Amanda out for one meal and it would undoubtedly put a smile back on Jason's face.

From now on he'd just avoid running into Amanda—set up some kind of schedule with her. "But then again, I wouldn't want a pretty lady to be forced to eat the food here—and I use the term loosely—for a third time in one day," Garth agreed. "It might just do her in."

"Great," Jason said. "I guess you ought to get going."

"Going? I just got here," Garth protested. "Don't you want to finish your game with Aman...ah...Mrs. Powers? I was supposed to finish reading that mystery to you tonight."

"I'm kind of tired, Dad. I don't think I'll be awake much longer." His yawn was expansive. And fake!

The kid belongs on a stage, Garth thought, biting his lip to keep from laughing. "Perhaps Mrs. Powers has other plans."

"Amanda. Her name's Amanda, Dad. Her friends called her Mandy when she was my age."

Garth looked at Amanda. Color had flooded her cheeks. Her violet eyes were wide with embarrassment, giving her a look of utter vulnerability. She looked like a Mandy at that moment—young and achingly sweet. "I guess we'd better go eat, Mandy," Garth said as he took her hand and led her, unresisting and obviously quite dazed, to the door.

Amanda stopped short and turned. "We'll call this

game a draw since you're too tired to keep playing. See you tomorrow.''

''Hey! I had you beat. I want a rematch!''

Amanda laughed and the sound vibrated right through Garth. ''Any time,'' she promised, then turned back toward him with a bright smile.

Amanda glanced at Garth as the car passed beneath a streetlight. He gripped the wheel tightly and a muscle throbbed in his jaw. The man radiated tension. Was it simply her presence or had some doctor told him something about Jason that they hadn't told her? Was this second remission over?

''Is Jason all right?'' she asked.

Garth smiled. It was the helpless sort that came in spite of pain and fear. Love was the only emotion Amanda could think of that could produce such an expression. ''He seemed fine to me,'' Garth answered. ''In rare form. He finally found a new pigeon to play Monopoly with *and* he got his way. We're having dinner together, aren't we?''

''I meant his health. Today's tests.''

Garth shook his head. ''We'll hear tomorrow on those. What about yours? Did you get any feel for whether you're a match or not?''

''There was a problem in the lab, so my tests were put off until tomorrow.'' They lapsed into an uncomfortable silence. ''If...ah...you'd rather not go to dinner with me, I'll understand.''

Garth blinked as if surprised that she'd draw such a conclusion from the silence that had stretched between them. ''Huh? Not go—? Oh, no.'' He sighed and pulled into the parking lot of an Italian restaurant. "I'm sorry if you misunderstood. It's been a lousy day. Maybe it's *you* who should rethink dinner with *me*."

"It's my being Jason's mother that has you this upset though, isn't it?"

Garth turned toward her. "It's the future and the past that have me tied in knots, not the present. None of this mess is your fault. Jason's your son. I meant what I said yesterday during the medical briefing. You're the victim in this. Jason, too. He's missed a lot of years with you because of what happened and now, even if he lives, he'll still lose the life he's known."

Garth got out of the car then and circled it to open her door, then directed her toward the restaurant. Amanda glanced up at his handsome profile and admitted the truth to herself. She was attracted to him, against all logic and sane judgment—against her promises to herself. This dinner together was definitely a bad idea.

But thoughts of past mistakes fled when she noticed Garth's troubled expression. It reminded her of something Jason had said earlier. *"I'm his reason for living."* Garth had said essentially the same thing the night he'd flown her to Philadelphia. He was ready to give up on the business he'd worked so hard to make succeed. Despite tough economic times and the odds against a small carrier succeeding in the northeast, Garth had made his dream come true. His dreams had apparently ended the day he'd confirmed her existence.

"Finding me doesn't have to mean you'll be out of his life," she told him as they took their seats.

"Jason would resent me if you just disappear. We need to find a way to—"

"Share him? Come on, Amanda. He has a long recovery ahead. He's not just a piece of baggage we can ship all over the country. You live in New Orleans. You have a job. Friends. A home. I live here. It's not as if I could drop over once or twice a week even though I'm a pilot."

"All my job in New Orleans meant to me after Jesse—I mean Jason—was born was a means of support. Even after he was taken, the job just paid for my search. My friends have drifted away because they were uncomfortable with my continuing to look for my son. Jason is my main concern. It can't be a good idea to take him away from all that's familiar to him."

"Are you saying you'd think of moving here?"

Before Amanda could answer, a waitress stepped up to their booth. Since Amanda had done no more than glance at the menu, she ordered spaghetti. Garth dittoed her order then looked at her, silently demanding an answer.

"I have no family," Amanda said softly. "I recently sold my house for money to continue the search for Jason." She looked down at the tablecloth. "I had yet to sign a lease on the new apartment I planned to move into and the company I work for has offices here. I might be able to get a transfer. It would be better for Jason to stay close to his doctors and your family...and...and you."

Garth stared at Amanda, clearly taken aback.

"You *don't* want him out of your life do you?" she asked.

Garth bristled, "Of course not, but—" His gaze drifted over her shoulder then back to her face. "I don't know if it's a good idea for us to have too much contact. Jason's been trying to…well…"

Amanda didn't bother to fight the smile that tugged at her lips. "How could I help but notice. He wants you to date, doesn't he?" she asked with a slight smile.

Garth chuckled helplessly. "You can't imagine. Ever since he noticed other kids had a mother and not a grandmom to take care of them. His first-grade teacher and I got on a first-name basis. Not because I took her out but because of the truly bizarre ways Jase had of getting me up to his school. The kid's fixated on getting me married. Frankly, it's not something I ever intend to do again. Women want more than I can give—feelings I can't give or believe in."

"Do you mean love?"

"That's a pretty, dressed-up name people have given lust and possessiveness."

Amanda grimaced. Her marriage hadn't been very happy, either. But Garth seemed to reject the very basis of marriage. She, on the other hand, still believed there was a man meant for her out there somewhere. But next time she would marry for companionship…friendship…not passion and attraction. Next time the man would be someone as committed to her faith as she was, not someone who might just give lip service to her Lord in order to lure her into marriage. She knew she never again wanted to tie her life to someone who didn't share her values. "I understand," she said. And she did understand why he felt what he did even though she didn't agree with his definition of love. Karen had really done a number on this man.

"No, no I don't think you do. Your marriage was a happy one. I'll bet Jess Powers was your childhood sweetheart."

"I was young when we met but that wasn't a guarantee of happiness," she hedged.

"No, but I married in haste and you know what that leads to. Karen was a flight attendant, beautiful and sophisticated. I wanted to believe what we had together was enough. We were married in a quick ceremony in Las Vegas between flights. I managed to break my mother's heart and ruin my life with one stupid decision that was based on lust."

"Your mother didn't approve of Karen." Their lives had run along such close parallel lines it was uncanny, though they had come away from their similar experiences with such different views on love. Amanda hoped Garth didn't also feel the same kind of attraction for her that she felt for him.

"Karen had an obsessive personality. Mom saw through her in minutes. Karen had decided to marry me so no lie was too big, even to pretending to be a different kind of person than she really was. She told so many lies that I couldn't wade through them after a while."

Amanda felt a chill. Yes, their lives had run very parallel. Right down to being fooled by the same woman. "She lied with truthful eyes," Amanda said. "I should know. I trusted her with my baby. I called the police minutes after I found them gone but I still couldn't really believe Keira had stolen him. I was holding her note and I still couldn't believe. She was my friend. She was my labor coach. She held me when I cried because Jess would never see him.''

''That's something we've both avoided talking about with each other since that night at your house,'' Garth said, looking pensive. ''I know this may seem strange but I need to know what happened. How she got away so clean. A baby is a real happening on an airline. They usually scream so loud I can sometimes hear them all the way in the cockpit. The air pressure bothers their ears.''

Amanda could see that Garth needed to hear what she'd gone through but she couldn't understand why. Perhaps he needed to know what had happened in Jason's life when he wasn't with either of them.

''It was a day just like any other,'' she began. ''I came home from work expecting to see the lights on in the house. But it was dark inside. And it gave me an odd feeling. Then the front door wasn't locked. There was no answer when I called out. They weren't in any of the day rooms. There was no message on the refrigerator explaining that she'd taken Jesse to the store or anywhere else. I started to really panic then. I thought that perhaps he'd gotten terribly sick and Keira had rushed him to the doctor's or a hospital. I ran into Jesse's room looking for evidence that she'd dressed him in a hurry. Or that he was sick. But most of his clothes were gone. Then I found the note and I called Jess's old captain. He notified the FBI immediately but it was already too late.''

''What did the note say?''

''That she needed a son. That there was no other way. She turned my life into a nightmare because she needed my son. So she just took him.'' Amanda swallowed hard. Even after all this time, after having miraculously found Jesse again, the pain, the unbearable panic and self-reproach of those first days still overwhelmed her.

"Karen told me she'd had the baby in New York City," Garth said.

Amanda shrugged, shaking off emotion, speaking calmly. "All the authorities were ever able to learn was that Keira had boarded a plane to Maine that morning at about the time I got to work. She rented a car that was abandoned in Michigan. There was never a trace of them after that. They had simply vanished."

"She must have gone to New York at some point because that was where she found out about the child who was born and died within a few weeks. She must have gotten a copy of his birth certificate. My detective says that's easy to do. When she showed up in Philly, she said Jason was six months old. I think he may have been older than she said. He walked early, talked early. But I guess I was a typical new father. My kid was brilliant."

"His birthday is August twenty-sixth," she said with a sad smile.

Garth sighed. "We've always celebrated it on November second."

"Why do you think she told you she'd given birth in New York? Suppose you had decided to check out her story. She might have been found out."

"Because she had been in New York. There was always some element of truth in her lies. The envelope with Jason's birth certificate in it was addressed to the name she claimed to have assumed when giv-

ing birth. It matched the mother's name on his birth
certificate and the father was listed as unknown.''
Garth looked up from fiddling with his salad. In his
eyes she saw something she couldn't define.

''Garth, what's wrong?''

''Even after all the lies, I believed her story of
taking an assumed name and leaving my name off
the birth certificate to punish me for wanting a divorce.'' Garth looked back down and stirred his
salad. ''My biggest disappointment when the marriage fell apart was that I'd probably never have a
child. And she knew it! Could I have been desperate
enough for a son that I turned a blind eye to the truth
when she presented me with one? I'll tell you something, Amanda. It haunts me to think I might have.''

''What did you do when you found out you
weren't Jason's father?''

''I was hurt, furious. I still had Karen's things in
the attic because I'd had my mother pack it all up
and store it there for Jason some day. Then I found
out she'd lied to me about being Jason's father. I
started going through it all, throwing it out. It was a
good thing Jason was in the hospital because I acted
like a maniac. Then I found the picture of you and
the baby.''

Garth rubbed his eyes. ''When I read the back, this
sick feeling hit me like a ton of bricks. I just stared
at it and sank down onto a box. The baby looked so
much like Jason. I hired a detective. He didn't tell
me right away but he started looking for the death
certificate on Jason—the real Jason. When he learned
that the boy had died within a month of his birth, we

knew Karen hadn't given birth to Jason at all. We started searching for you."

Amanda found herself once more choking back emotion. But this time it was Garth's pain she felt. "So, how can you say you turned a blind eye? You did the right thing as soon as you knew."

Garth gave her a sad smile, one absent of joy. "Now if the FBI just believes in me half as much as you and my mother seem to. It's my word against a dead woman's that I wasn't involved, you realize. I was in New Orleans with her when your husband was killed. That could look pretty bad. Even if they believe me, they could ground me until they're sure. I can't afford that right now."

Amanda grabbed at a chance to add a little levity to the discussion. She really thought Garth needed it right then. "Ground you? How about taking away TV for a week?" she teased with a chuckle in her voice.

Garth rolled his eyes and grinned. Amanda breathed a grateful sigh that she'd been able to lighten his mood. He shook his finger at her, teasing her back. "It is not polite to ridicule a man's professional buzzwords." Then he sobered. "I'm a pilot, Amanda. I have to stay in the air. I can't afford not to fly."

Unconsciously, Amanda reached out and covered his hand. She was immediately sorry she had. It was all there. Everything Jess had made her feel and more. The need to comfort. The need to be near. That wonderful, undeniable electric jolt at the slightest contact. But for Garth there seemed no such reaction. He only looked worried. Her compassion warred with her fear of repeating past mistakes. Compassion won, as usual. This situation could be serious for Garth. "Did you see an attorney?"

"He said he'd go to court and get the judge to allow me to fly because it's my livelihood if the FBI does ground me but it could take days or a week just to get the hearing scheduled."

"Garth, none of that's going to happen. I'll talk to the FBI agent who's handling the case and make sure he believes you. I don't think you need to worry about it, but while we're talking about your business may I ask you a question?"

When Garth gave her a noncommittal shrug, Amanda decided to take it as a yes. "Is Liberty Express in financial trouble?" she asked.

Garth dragged his free hand through his hair, then shrugged again. "I've got medical insurance but it doesn't cover everything. The foundation my employees and family have set up for Jason has helped but…" Garth grimaced. "My house carries a second mortgage now. The business, too."

Amanda felt a little guilty for her initial thoughts on seeing Liberty Express's offices the morning of her arrival. Not only had he not planned to use his wealth to keep her son, he'd already spent it all to save Jason's life.

Her heart softened even more toward him. She hated to see him weighed down with so many problems. But then if there was one thing she'd learned since Jesse's abduction, it was that life was rarely fair. Garth had learned that lesson, too. She could tell by the way he'd spoken the night before. She hated to see him learn it again and again.

There was a pause while Amanda gathered her courage. They had other things to discuss. There were things *she* had to know and understand. And one request to make of him. "About Liberty Express, please don't do anything about selling it. Now is an emotional time for all of us. Promise me that you won't make any decisions until Jason's well. You might later regret anything you do."

Garth didn't think she understood. "I promise to think about it. But you have to understand that when I started Liberty it was for the future but now I don't have a son to pass it on to. Without that there's no reason to keep hanging on to a dying dream. I may as well go back to measuring success in dollars alone."

Amanda opened her mouth to comment but stopped. "I'm glad you'll think over your decision. Now." She took a deep breath. "About Jason. I'd like to talk to you about him. A-about the leukemia. I have questions."

Garth clenched his teeth. He couldn't take much more tonight. He'd made a big mistake asking her to relate what she knew of Jason's kidnapping and its aftermath. He'd thought hearing about her past pain would somehow lessen the agony he was going through at present but it hadn't. Instead, he felt not only his pain but hers as well and he felt responsible for both.

He was sure the questions she needed answered were questions she had every right to ask. But he hated to think about the past year, let alone talk about it. Memories of the terror he'd faced when learning of Jason's illness and of all the suffering Jason been through since flooded his memory. And all he had to hang on to was the hope that he'd made the right choices. And that was no comfort at all. One remission had ended, hadn't it?

He was so afraid he'd made a wrong decision about the chemo and that he'd put Jason through all that for nothing. It was that fear that ruled when he practically snarled his own set of questions. "What exactly would you like me to tell you? That the first round of chemo failed? That it decimated Jason? That I'm responsible for putting him through all that pain for nothing? That I approved it a second time because I couldn't face losing him?" Garth knew his tone was sharp and cutting but he was helpless to change it. He was bleeding, too.

He watched Amanda take a careful, deep breath before she responded to his spate of questions. "Actually, it isn't really his medical treatment I have questions about but the way you talk to him and some of the things I've heard you say to him."

The blood pounded in Garth's head. "Are you questioning the way I've raised Jason thus far?"

Amanda sat straighter in her seat and now her eyes blazed. "I'm not questioning a thing! I was trying to compliment you! I think it's admirable that you'd tell him about heaven when I've heard you question God out of his hearing."

"Of course I question. I've held him while he vomited for hours on end and got so weak he couldn't roll over himself to keep from choking. I've watched him go from being the best ball player on his team to not being able to lift a bat. One day I found him gluing his hair to the edges of his hat so none of the other kids would know his hair had fallen out.''

''And that's why you joke with him about it?''

Garth nodded. ''Because, sometimes, if you don't laugh, you cry. Laughter keeps things in perspective for him. It helps him see how unimportant his appearance is if the chemo will save his life. Fear is a big enemy for Jason. To help him cope, I told him some of the fables from the Bible that my mother and father told me.''

Amanda reached out and grasped his hand with hers and Garth glanced away as his heart skipped a beat. He would not acknowledge any attraction he felt toward Jason's mother. It was emotional suicide.

''They're not fables, Garth. They're promises and guidelines,'' she whispered, that soft Southern lilt in her voice soothing his jangled nerves and awakening feelings he feared to acknowledge.

He took a deep, steadying breath, retreating to familiar ground. He went a round with his mother at least once a week. ''I challenged you to explain God and His selective blessings to me already. When you have an answer, we'll talk about it. In the meantime, if you want to help Jason you can help him keep the balance he's achieved. It's a delicate one.''

''I understand and I'll try to help him fight, too.'' Amanda looked past her own pain to the same feelings reflected in Garth's eyes. His pain was worse, though. It had to be. He didn't believe God's hand was on the situation. She wouldn't push further now. It had been a long day for both of them. ''Tell me about before. Tell me about Jason growing up.''

Garth's smile was sad but quickly became wistful

and often joyous as he talked about the boy they both called son. Their shared mood was pensive and serene until he climbed in the car beside her and she gave him her motel's address.

"What on earth possessed you to take a room there? I thought you were at the Ronald McDonald House near Children's."

Amanda stiffened at his tone. "As they say, there was no room at the inn and this is the only place I can afford for an extended period. It isn't that bad."

"Amanda, please—it's awful, and you know it!"

Amanda blushed. "It is a bit seedy. I'll concede that point, but I can afford it."

"You're checking out tonight," he ordered.

"And where, pray tell, do you think I'll sleep? I told you, it's all I can afford. Once the sale of the house is complete I'll move to something more suitable."

"I won't have Jason's mother staying in a place like that. You can stay at my house," Garth countered.

"I can't stay at your house. It wouldn't be right."

"For goodness sake, woman, you're in Philadelphia, not some judgmental small town. Who do you think would care? And don't give me that tired old business about it not being a good witness to your beliefs. Besides that—I live with my mother!"

Amanda giggled at his indignation and, though she still had some concerns, she gave in. It would only be for a short time. "All right, all right. Since your mother will be there, I'll stay till I can get a transfer to the Philadelphia branch worked out or the sale of the house goes through. Does that suit you?"

Garth pursed his lips and nodded but he had a strange look in his eyes. Almost as if he regretted his invitation.

"I could probably afford something a bit better if you'd rather I look around tonight," she countered, not wanting to be more of a burden on him than she already was. Just her presence in Philadelphia, near Jason, must be almost more than he could bear. Now the woman who was going to take his son away would be staying in his house. He couldn't want that.

"I wouldn't have invited you if I didn't want you here." Garth said. He muttered something that she could have sworn sounded a lot like, "That's the problem," but she couldn't be sure because it was lost in the noise of the engine starting. Praying that she'd heard wrong, she dismissed the idea. The same temptation couldn't possibly be visited upon her twice in one lifetime.

Could it?

Chapter Three

Garth grabbed Amanda's suitcase out of the trunk and led the way up the front walk from the sweeping drive. He tried to look at his house with the eyes of someone used to the French Quarter, Southern plantations and shotgun houses with homey wraparound porches. His two-hundred-year-old, three-story, stone colonial in the suburbs of Philadelphia spoke of Americana, dignity and grace. Her house was surrounded by colorful flowering bushes and perennials, his by a stone wall, sedate shrubbery and ancient trees.

Did she think it looked pretentious and cold? Or did she see what he had the first time he'd seen it—a home. To Garth, the house was a sign of everything he'd had as a child—and then lost. He'd found what he'd lost here with Jason and his mother, Frieda. For six years these four stone walls had meant home and security. Now he'd lose it once again. Oh, he'd still have the house but the home he'd built within its sturdy exterior would be gone.

The outdoor lights came on and lit up the grounds and the house itself. Amanda gasped. "Oh, Garth, this is lovely. I feel as if I just stepped into Colonial America."

"It's almost that old," he told her, smiling. He knew he shouldn't let himself care what Amanda thought but her approval mattered. And that meant she was trouble. He wanted Amanda in his life and he had no business thinking or feeling that way. He had to be crazy. Why had he invited her here? He'd promised himself that he'd stay away from her! How could he avoid someone who was living under his own roof?

The front door opened, drawing Garth's attention off his troubled thoughts. His mother stepped out. She was a small, gray-haired, gentle-looking woman but Garth, at six-two, still tried not to cross swords with her. He cringed inwardly. He'd thought of his mother only as a chaperon to ease Amanda's worries. What his mother was going to be was trouble with a capital *T*.

Amanda was the woman who would take away the grandson his mother had helped raise from infancy. There'd be resentment and anger at first. Frieda was a mother hen of the first water. But that would only be at first. Because Amanda was also what his mother would call a good Christian woman. And Frieda Jorgensen had been trying to find a woman like Amanda for him for years. Most women would shun Amanda indefinitely but his mother was not most women. She would more likely see blending of their lives as the will of the Lord—the Lord she vehemently espoused to him at every opportunity. A Lord he no longer served.

"Garth, what are you doing home so early? Nothing's wrong with Jason, I hope," she said when they reached her.

"Jason's fine. More than fine," he answered, thinking of the self-satisfied grin Jason had worn when they'd left for dinner. Garth took a fortifying breath and tried to get ready for the fallout his foolish offer to Amanda of a place to stay was going to cause. He stepped to the side, ushering Amanda forward. "Mom, this is Amanda Powers."

"Oh." That one syllable was so packed full of fear and worry that Amanda stepped back. Her foot slid into the edge of the flower garden and she lost her balance. It was instinct that made him wrap his arms around her waist so she wouldn't fall. But it wasn't instinct that made his heartbeat accelerate. Garth's gaze flew from the top of Amanda's head to his eagle-eyed mother. She propped a hand on her hip and raised an eyebrow, her forehead wrinkling with contemplation. Garth groaned silently, afraid she'd seen his reaction to Amanda's nearness. He hoped against hope that there would be no time for her and Amanda to get into a discussion of personal belief systems.

His mother smiled. "Welcome, Amanda. Call me Frieda."

Garth closed his eyes and sighed. He'd seen it coming, hadn't he? Unfortunately he'd seen it too late. His mother knew how Amanda's nearness had affected him. And now his goose would be cooked once they got to know one another. Why hadn't he just offered to pay for better accommodations for her elsewhere?

"I'm so pleased to meet you," his mother continued. "Jason's told me all about you."

"Jason told you about me?"

"Oh, indeed. He called me for just that reason. You two got on like a house afire, I hear. I'm glad someone's treated you well. Just for the record, I wondered what had gotten into my son when he came home without you last night," his mother continued. "I suppose you stayed at the Ronald McDonald House."

Amanda laughed. "Actually, there was no room there. I stayed at a motel but Garth didn't think it was safe. I wasn't entirely comfortable there but it did have a wonderful little church just down the street. I went to services there last night."

"Wednesday night services? How nice!" his mother replied with a wide, Cheshire cat smile. "You just come right on in."

Garth groaned. Well, that hadn't taken long!

Amanda turned and looked at him. She was so confused it was almost funny. Almost. But not quite. It had taken all of ten seconds to throw a second, and more accomplished matchmaker in the mix. Worse, by ten the next morning, she'd be in league with Jason. "Watch her," he whispered in Amanda's ear. "We usually wind up doing exactly what she wants. She might look like a pushover but she steers us all with an iron hand."

"Garth Colbey Jorgensen, what tales are you telling this young lady?"

"No tales. Just warning her about you, Mom."

"What could you warn Amanda about where I'm concerned? I'm just a nice old lady. Come in, dear. I'll see about your room."

An hour later Garth was in the study adjacent to his room. He was ready for bed but he had a few things to work on and he was getting nothing done. The events of the evening and Amanda were on his mind.

He sighed heavily as he remembered his mother's last question as they'd entered the house. What was he warning Amanda about? Nice old lady? His mother was already at work! That's what he was worried about! The gleam that had come into her eyes had still been there when he'd parted company with her and Amanda.

Ten minutes later Garth realized he was pacing and that his mother could hear the floor creaking. He dropped quickly into his desk chair, trying to focus on the report he had to finish. Liberty Express was always a welcome distraction.

Garth was deep into facts and figures when, from just down the hall, the silvery notes of a song rose above the muted sound of the running shower. Amanda's voice was as sweet as the lyrics she sang.

She'd promised to call the FBI agent who was in charge of Jason's case and add her endorsement to his character. Why couldn't she have been vindictive instead of so understanding? He'd at least have a chance of guarding his heart if she were.

Amanda slipped beneath the covers and let her head sink into the feather pillow. She closed her eyes and inhaled the smell of sheets dried outdoors in the sun. They smelled of fresh air and the housewifely pleasure of crisp, clean beds. She'd never take that wonderful aroma for granted again. To think foolish pride had almost kept her from such a simple pleasure! "Thank you for this special night, Lord," she whispered. "And for the simple pleasures of life."

Her eyes sprang open at the sound of footsteps in the hall. They ended with a crash and a split second later a very male hiss followed. Garth! Her peace fled as thoughts of him flooded her mind.

Wasn't this just like life? Garth had experienced the joy of raising her son for the past six years and to envy and even resent him for that would have been only human. Yet, after meeting him she had a hard time not liking him. Amanda shook her head ruefully. Be honest, she told herself, you more than like him. Even though they were poles apart on fundamental issues, she was more strongly drawn to him than she had been even to Jess Powers. Why did she have to be attracted to the one man in the universe she shouldn't be? He didn't know the Lord. In fact, he was downright hostile about Him. And he'd sounded alarmingly like a man who measured his worth on his success—just the way Jess had. There was also his adamant belief that *love* was a word used to dress up domination, need or lust. Yet even with all those strikes against him, he was so very attractive—everything she'd promised to avoid and then some.

She'd tried to tell herself that the feeing that arced between them was because of their mutual love for Jason. But that was a lie. She'd felt something stir in her heart when she'd fallen against him and into his arms on the front walk earlier. And what she'd felt had nothing to do with mutual feelings for Jason.

And then there was Garth's mother. The older woman had clearly decided to throw Amanda and Garth together. And her reasons were easy to understand. Mrs. Jorgensen didn't want to lose Jason and what better way to keep him right where he was? It made perfect sense.

What was she to do? First, Jason had innocently pushed her and Garth together for dinner. Then Mrs. Jorgensen, not so innocently, stepped into the act with hints about how wonderful a husband Garth would make the right woman and what a wonderful father he was. And Garth had seemed embarrassed at the hospital when Jason had all but strong-armed him into asking her to dinner. He clearly didn't want to be near her—which she should understand and even be grateful for. Instead, she was insulted. Which she shouldn't be. But was.

It was all too much!

Amanda rolled over and deliberately thought of what tomorrow would bring. Another visit with her son. Her tests. Needles! No, that was worse.

She went back to prayer but the last thought that drifted through her head was that she'd be less afraid of the tests if Garth were with her during them.

Garth checked his watch as he waited for the traffic to clear. He glanced up at the hospital. The sun glinted off the windows and the light-colored facade. He didn't dread it today. He felt good. Better than he had in months. The results were in and Amanda was as close a match as they were likely to find. He couldn't wait to tell her and see her reaction. Hear her reaction.

He shook his head. Amanda was the most curious mix of childlike exuberance and femininity he'd ever encountered. She giggled when she was happy but stoically hid her fears and sorrows. She relied on her Lord for strength with a child's faith but was tough as old shoe leather when she had to be.

Garth stepped into the street and rushed forward. He couldn't wait to see her. It wasn't wise but he could fight just so many battles at one time. Five minutes, two corridors and one elevator ride later, Garth pushed open the door to Jason's room. He was surprised to find Jason looking disheartened. "Hey, buddy. Why the long face? That cut giving you fits?"

"Na. I hardly feel it. She didn't come see me, Dad."

"Who?"

"Mrs. Powers. I think I may have made her mad. I mean, everyone isn't as good as you about losing games to a kid."

Garth sat on the edge of the bed. "She wasn't the least bit upset. In fact, she likes you so much that today she had a test done to see if she could be a donor for that transplant Dr. Matt has been talking so much about."

"She did? Wow." Jason's eyes lit up but just as quickly the flame of happiness dimmed and his face screwed up in a look of total consternation. "But she hates needles."

"So?"

"I mean she *really* hates them, Dad. Yesterday she got all white and her hands started shaking and it was *me* getting stuck. The nurse made her sit down and put her head between her knees. I sure hope she didn't get too scared.''

Garth eyed Jason, trying to decide if Amanda was really as terrified as Jason said or if his son was attempting to set another matchmaking trap. Garth frowned as a thought filtered through the suspicion.

''She didn't come to see you at *all* today?'' he asked Jason who shook his head, looking sad and worried.

And now Garth was worried about her, too. Wild horses wouldn't keep Amanda away from her son. It bothered Garth how much he wanted to assure himself that she was all right. ''Would it make you feel better if I went and made sure she's okay?''

Jason perked up in a flash. ''Would you? I really want to make sure she's okay. It would be my fault if she wasn't. Thanks, Dad.''

Feeling like a man on his way to an execution—his own—Garth left Jason and went looking for Amanda. He stopped first at the nurses' station near Jason's room. ''Excuse me, Cindy,'' he said to the perky blonde behind the desk.

Cindy Kelly looked up from the chart in her hand. ''Mr. Jorgensen, what can I do for you?''

''I wondered if you'd heard anything about that new volunteer who's spent so much time with Jason. Amanda Powers. She had tests today to see if she could be a donor for Jason. Ah…he missed seeing her.''

''Amanda Powers? She's resting down the hall. Room 302. She went into shock during the tests. She's fine but—''

"Shock? From tests? What did they do to her?"

Nurse Kelly's smile was indulgent. "She's fine. She fainted. That's all. Really. But I'll go—"

Garth spun away and bolted toward 302. He entered the room as quietly as he could, not wanting to wake her if she was asleep. She was, her blond hair spread like gold across the pillow. He longed to feel the silkiness of those strands slip through his fingers. He raked his hand through his own hair instead. In sleep, her face was peaceful as if she had put her fears and troubles aside for a while. She was beautiful.

Garth reached out to touch her but pulled his hand back just short of contact. He wanted too much from this woman. He cared too much about her, too. But Amanda Powers was not for him. A tap on the door drew Garth's attention.

He opened it to find the young nurse, Cindy Kelly. He followed her into the hall. "I wasn't sure I was supposed to tell you she was in there. Her being Jason's mother and all." Garth felt the blood drain out of his head. Cindy Kelly reached out to him. "Mr. Jorgensen, are you all right?"

Garth gritted his teeth and grabbed the door frame in a death grip. She took a wary step backward and Garth followed her into the hall. "Jason can't find out," he warned. "We were told not to tell him."

Looking perplexed, the nurse nodded. "I'll make sure that no one tells him. We'll even instruct the cleaning people since it's all over the hospital grapevine."

Garth stood stunned as the nurse hurried back toward her station. Amanda had told their secret! Feeling angry and betrayed, he shoved the door to Room 302 open again and stalked to the bed. He looked at the woman in the bed with new eyes and wondered why he'd been such a fool to believe her willingness to wait. Would he never learn?

"Amanda," he barked.

Amanda's eyes flew open as she shot up in the bed. She could just make out the scowling face of the man who'd haunted her dreams. But he'd haunted them with a smile not a frown. "Garth?" She looked around at the darkened room. "Oh, goodness! How long did I sleep?"

"I'm not sure. I came looking for you because Jason missed your visit today. He was worried when I told him about your test."

Her son had *missed* her and he'd *worried* about her. Elation spread through her but just as quickly it vanished. Amanda felt a keen disappointment take over her spirit when Garth's annoyance penetrated the after-fog of sleep. Jason, not Garth, had cared. In fact, she seemed to have angered him.

Pushing dangerous notions and foolish wishes for Garth's goodwill aside, Amanda stared at his tight expression. Was Garth jealous that Jason had worried about her? Or just angry that she'd carelessly allowed Jason to become upset?

"I'm sorry he's worried," she said as she swung her legs out of the bed and stood. "I'll go see him and get out of the way so you can have your visit."

"Are you sure you can hold your tongue with *him* at least?" Garth snapped.

"Hold my tongue about what? What on earth are you growling about?"

"They all know that you're Jason's mother, Amanda. Just how many people have you told?" he accused.

Amanda sat back down, her knees collapsing under her. She stared at Garth in shock but then righteous anger flooded her. "How dare you accuse me of spreading my relationship to Jason around? I don't know how anyone found out but it wasn't from my lips. I've searched too long for my child to endanger him now!"

"Then how did they all find out?"

"How should I know? All I know is that I haven't told anyone." Even in the low light it was obvious from his mutinous expression that Garth doubted her. Amanda's outrage grew as she shoved her feet into her shoes. "You don't believe me. You really don't believe me! You know, Garth, trust has to go both ways. When you told me you didn't have anything to do with the kidnapping, I believed *you* and you were a stranger! You should know enough about me by now to know how much I love Jason, yet there you stand accusing me of doing something to hurt him. You have a heck of nerve and a warped view of people." Amanda didn't wait for a reply but stormed out the door.

Garth followed her slowly to Jason's room and entered quietly. Amanda had already taken a position at the foot of the bed and had just finished setting up the Monopoly game board on the dinner tray table. He gritted his teeth. She was supposed to have a quick visit and leave. He sauntered in and sat on the bed next to Jason. This was his time. He didn't have much of it left with Jason and he wanted every precious second. It was selfish but he was too mad to care.

Jason looked up and smiled. "Hi, Dad. Want to play with us?"

Amanda swallowed nervously when she saw Garth's expression but stiffened her spine and with it her resolve. He might look mad enough to chew her up and spit her out but she wouldn't be intimidated. How dare he accuse her? This might be his time to visit but so what! He'd had all the years she should have had with her son already. And she could still lose Jason before she'd ever really gotten him back. Let him learn to share!

Garth's eyes bore into hers in a silent signal. *You're trespassing.*

She glared right back. *Tough.*

"Sure, I'll play," Garth answered, then added almost defiantly, "You're the hat, right, *son?*"

Jason tipped his cap and laughed before handing Garth a marker. "And you're the car. Right?" Her son smiled at her. "It's as close to a plane as he can get. Dad likes speed. What's your choice? I've got a cute dog here or Grandmom always picks the thimble. Hey, how about the iron? You're a woman. There's a wheelbarrow and a horse, too, but they're guy things. Right, Dad?" Jason teased, elbowing Garth in the ribs.

Amanda felt her muscles relax. She couldn't be in the same room with her son and stay angry. "You little chauvinist! I'll have you know I hate ironing. I'll take the horse. I used to ride a lot. My grandfather had a little farm and a big old gelding named General. I used to ride whenever I had a chance."

Jason frowned as he counted out Garth's fifteen hundred dollars start money from the bank. "What kind of horse is a gelding?"

Garth chuckled and gestured to Amanda indicating that the question was all hers. She cleared her throat, determined not to let the nature of the question ruffle her. This was her first chance to be a parent to her son in seven years. "Well, you see stallions are hard to handle. So, at a certain point, they're altered and then they're called geldings. You see?" She clapped her hands together. "Let's get on with the game. Shall we?" she suggested, feeling as if Garth had set her up.

Garth went on the attack. Monopoly ceased to be a game to him. He played ruthlessly. It quickly became evident that this was personal. Under the jovial face he'd put on for Jason, he was still furious with her. Amanda felt sorry for his real competitors as she paid her rent for landing at his Park Place hotel.

"You owe me ten more dollars, Mrs. Powers," Garth demanded as he counted the currency she'd just handed him. "Can't you count or are you a cheat, too?"

"Dad? It's just a game. That's what you always tell me."

Garth looked for a split second as if he might snap at Jason. Even though his expression changed in the blink of an eye, she quickly handed over her last ten dollars and stood up. She couldn't in good conscience let Garth's anger at her boil over onto Jason. "Listen, guys, that did it for me tonight. I think I'll grab a cab and run on home. May the best man win. I'll get by to see you tomorrow, Jason. And Mr. Jorgensen, from now on, I'll make sure I'm gone before you arrive. I'm sorry I encroached on your private time with your son tonight.''

Garth watched in stunned silence as Amanda disappeared.

"Did you have a bad day or what?" Jason asked, glaring at him and tearing his cap off.

Garth grimaced. "I think *or what.* I suppose you want me to go apologize." Jason nodded.

He did have things to discuss with Amanda and he didn't want his mother to be party to that discussion. Garth stood, not happy to find himself leaving so early. He deeply resented losing a second night with Jason. "I'll be back and maybe bring Mrs. Powers with me."

Jason crossed his arms in a stubborn pose. "Only if you're calling her Amanda again."

Garth hurried down the hall in time to see Amanda's blond hair flow behind her around a corner. He heard the stairwell door slam shut as he rounded the corner. Garth ran after her down the steps, calling several times but Amanda just kept racing ahead. Garth made it to the exit door just after she did. He reached past her head and slapped the door shut just as she started to pull it open.

Amanda froze. She wasn't frightened. At least not physically. Garth wouldn't hurt a fly but she knew he would protect Jason no matter what the threat. She shivered. He thought she'd tried to hurt Jason by revealing her relationship to him. She refused to turn around, somehow knowing she'd lose something vital if she did.

They stood there for a long minute with Amanda

feeling Garth's closeness to her core but determined to ignore it. Garth took her by the shoulders, finally, and turned her to face him, breaking the stalemate.

Their eyes locked, hers combative, his filled with regret. "I'm sorry," he whispered. His caressing gaze robbed her of her anger. "I should've known you'd never do anything to hurt Jason."

Amanda found she couldn't look away. "You have a lot on your mind."

"I'm tired. I'm worried about—" Garth's fingertips trailed across her cheek and Amanda felt a spark pass between them. "No. No, there's no excuse," he whispered as he bent his head. "Just like there's no excuse for this." His lips found Amanda's in a gentle salutation. "No excuse at all." He kissed her again, his kiss expressing his longing yet no less gentle. The spark blazed into something so powerful it left Amanda weak and shaken. Garth broke the kiss but his arms engulfed her and pressed her close. "This is wrong. I know it but I just don't care." His lips covered hers again.

And Amanda realized what it was she'd been afraid she would lose if she turned around and looked at Garth.

Her heart.

Chapter Four

The stairwell door suddenly smacked into Amanda's back and threw her even more tightly against Garth's solid frame, the dangerous moment thankfully shattered. As one, they moved to the side like automatons, both shocked and a little horrified, though for their own diverse reasons.

A small ferret of a man in a white lab coat squeezed through the door. It was obvious that he had a good idea what he'd interrupted. "Sorry," he said with a knowing grin as he stared at Amanda.

Amanda remembered him from the lab when her tests were done. She remembered the way he'd stared at her and that he was a terrible gossip. She ducked her head, feeling a flush rush up her neck to heat her face. She had no doubt that he would add this latest story to the other, making her and Garth tomorrow's top subject on the hospital grapevine. He might even be the person who'd told everyone about her true relationship to Jason.

Garth stepped between them and blocked her view of the interloper. "Sorry," the man said again as he scurried up the stairs. This time he sounded as if he meant it.

Once the man was gone, Garth turned and reached for her again. Amanda sucked a strangled breath, afraid of the things he'd made her feel but wanting to feel them all the same. She'd never felt anything with her husband that even resembled what she felt minutes ago in Garth's arms. And that reckless need for Jess had nearly destroyed her, she reminded herself. She couldn't risk this. She had to fight it because feelings like these couldn't be trusted—couldn't be good.

She had to remember the pain she'd felt losing Jess to his obsession with worldly adoration and his death in its pursuit. She had vowed never to risk so dangerous an involvement again. And to break that rule for a man like Garth—a man who so openly disdained her faith and sought after worldly success—would make her ten times a fool. And Amanda would be no one's fool again. She'd found it wasn't a role she liked playing.

As he stepped closer, Amanda planted her hand in the middle of his chest. "You're right," she said. "This is wrong."

Garth stared down at her. Regret and something that shouted loneliness flashed in his eyes before they went hard and cold. He snatched his hands off her as if burned and stepped away. "Sorry," he said.

Amanda wasn't sure what he'd apologized for. The kiss, the interruption or her refusal to accept another. She wasn't sure she wanted to know, so she didn't ask. "It was just a kiss," she said and turned toward the door silently confessing the lie.

"Just?" he asked, clearly dubious.

She turned back to confront him only because she knew it needed to be done. "It can't be more." Amanda almost hoped he'd disagree.

Garth's eyes narrowed, assessing her. Amanda met his gaze with determination. His jaw tensed. "Whatever you say."

Amanda turned to leave again but Garth stayed her with a hand on her shoulder. She backed away, determined to keep him at a distance. "What?"

Garth's hand dropped and curled at his side before relaxing. "Jason wants us to come back," he admitted. "I'm in the doghouse with him for growling at you."

"Is he upset?"

"No. More like determined." Garth shrugged, his grin a bit sheepish and very reluctant as he buried his hands in his pockets. It was an expression she was quickly coming to associate with his reaction to Jason's precociousness. "I'm to return with you and be addressing you as Amanda if I know what's good for me. He can be a tough little guy when he digs in his heels."

"And it's equally tough on you to tell him no just now."

"Yeah," Garth admitted. "But he's right this time, even though he doesn't know why I acted the way I did. I really am sorry about the way I treated you upstairs. I know you care about Jason as much as I do. I shouldn't have doubted you but I have a hard time trusting since Karen. Come back, please."

Amanda didn't want hard feelings between them any more than she wanted the ones she'd felt when he'd kissed her. She nodded and followed him up the stairs to Jason's room. He was sitting with his legs and arms crossed, waiting like a Middle Eastern potentate when they entered.

Garth tried to be firm. "I asked *Amanda* to come back but don't think I did it because you told me to. It's you who obeys me, remember?" Jason lost a bit of the superior look in his eyes and nodded. "There was something I had to talk to both of you about," Garth continued as he took hold of Jason's hand. He smiled. "Your last tests were the best they've ever been, son, and—"

"I feel great, too. Does that mean I can come home again?"

Garth shook his head. "'Fraid not. You have to stay here because Amanda's test results are in, too. We've got a near perfect match, kid."

Jason's gaze flew from Garth to her. A grin split his face but his eyes were nearly worshipful. Amanda felt tears well up when he reached out and took her hand with his free one. Amanda glanced at Garth who studied their clasped hands then her face with sober eyes. It hadn't escaped Amanda's notice, either, that Jason was an undeniable link between them.

"So, now they bring in the heavy guns Doctor Matt told me about?" Jason asked. The trepidation in his tone drew the attention of both adults. Jason's smile had faded and there was apprehension in his eyes.

"I'm afraid so," Garth warned with a grimace.

Amanda had thought Jason and Garth would both be elated. "What heavy guns?" she asked.

"They'll start the chemo again plus do full body irradiation so that, when they do the transplant, your stem cells will replace his. Remember? We talked about this. Then when his body makes blood, it'll be cancer free."

"Will you be here more often like you were before?" Jason asked Garth.

"I'll be here as much as I can be. Grandmom will be here with you, too, and maybe Amanda could come more often. You wouldn't mind, would you, Amanda?"

"I'd be glad to visit more often. Jason's my favorite patient."

"It'll be worse than before, won't it?" Jason asked.

Garth held out his arms and Jason let go of her hand so he could nestle into Garth's embrace. "Dr. Hernandez doesn't think it necessarily will be. They're going to try a new drug to keep you from getting too sick. Hey, cheer up. This is good news."

Garth glanced at Amanda. It was obvious that she hadn't really understood all the transplant would entail. He knew she'd been told but now he remembered that no one had explained just how sick it would make Jason. He could see she was upset and unable to do what she wanted—to hug Jason the way he could in his role as Jason's father. It was unfair to her that he was free to offer comfort to her son but for the life of him he couldn't think of a way to include her.

They stayed with Jason until after ten when he

finally fell asleep. Then they tiptoed out of the room. "What happens now?" Amanda asked as they headed for the elevator.

"They'll begin the chemo and radiation tomorrow. Jason will be in isolation pretty soon because he'll be prey to any bacteria or viruses that come along. He'll get weaker because the infusion therapy will wipe out his blood cells. He'll hold down less food and eventually go on IV feeding entirely. It'll be rough going but it'll be worth it when it works." Garth stared at Amanda and answered the question in her eyes. "It has to work."

Amanda spent the next morning with Jason, then she went to the Philadelphia branch of her company to see if she could secure a transfer. Her timing couldn't have been better. The same job she did in New Orleans would be available in the Philadelphia office. Highly recommended by her boss back in Louisiana, Amanda soon found herself welcome at the Pennsylvania office. That left her with a four-month leave of absence to spend with Jason.

She couldn't wait to share her news with Garth. The ease with which she was able to transfer to Philadelphia had to have been heaven-sent. But Amanda's elation burst like a pin-stuck balloon when she stood in Jason's doorway and found Garth holding Jason's head as he vomited. He looked so small and even paler than he had before. Helpless. Exhausted.

Amanda fought tears as she listened while Garth spoke in soothing tones to their son. At that moment, Amanda realized that Jason was *their* son. Garth was as much his father as she was his mother and always would be. She would never have her baby all to herself again.

Just then Garth noticed her in the doorway. Their eyes met and he stiffened as if he'd seen into her heart to the resentment and jealousy she felt. But Garth's eyes betrayed him, as well. In the split second before he masked his thoughts in the face of her bitterness, she read so much worry and pain that she backed out of the room, ashamed.

She ran. She ran from the past. She ran from the future. But most of all, she ran from the present because she didn't know what else to do. There were too many things happening. Too many feelings bombarding her heart.

Amanda sought refuge in the hospital chapel. Drawn there by the need for the kind of comfort that only He could give, she begged for guidance and the strength to deal with all that life had suddenly thrown at her. She did what she'd learned at her mother's knee. She sat in the quiet, and listened. Not to herself but for a still quieter voice. She waited for Him to speak to her.

Amanda couldn't hide from the truth, sitting before her Lord. Her upset wasn't caused by Jason's illness. The leukemia caused fear and worry but not this churning turmoil. No. That was all tied up in Garth.

It was a very human emotion to feel resentment toward the man who'd had all the good years of Jason's life. It was what most people would call a normal reaction. But she knew feelings of resentment were wrong. Those emotions flashed through her anyway even as she fought them. They were feelings and emotions she didn't even want to feel, because of the kind of person Garth had turned out to be.

Garth was a good man. A decent and caring man who'd probably been hurt just as badly by Karen Jorgensen as Amanda herself had. He'd been good for Jason. She couldn't have asked for a better father for him, except for his lack of faith in God. And he even seemed to hide that from the boy.

But none of that was the overwhelming problem that had set her into flight from Jason and Garth. The problem was that she was drawn to Garth for her sake and not Jason's. And that frightened her.

The only solution seemed to be that she had to keep Garth out of her life as much as possible. He just made her *feel* too much and she'd made that mistake once already with Jess. And if that weren't enough, she had no way of knowing if Garth was drawn to her for herself or her claim to Jason. Amanda wondered if even Garth knew.

"Amanda," Garth said from the chapel doorway, "are you all right?"

Amanda felt the now familiar stirring deep in her soul at the sound of his voice. She stood and turned to face the first man she could love since her son's father. The flashing memory of a flag-draped coffin, a sea of blue uniforms, the smell of thousands of carnations and the sound of a twenty-one gun salute chased away any thoughts of falling in love again. It was just too dangerous with a man like Garth. Too familiar. Around him she really did feel too much.

"I'm fine," she lied. "It was a shock seeing him like that. He was fine this morning."

"I feel as if I lied to him. The antinausea drug isn't working with the new program. It's going to be bad."

Amanda hugged herself, her empty arms aching. All the resentment flooded her again. "I can't stand this. I want to hold him! I'm his mother but to him I'm just a kindly stranger, not someone to turn to for comfort."

"You're much more, Amanda. You're giving him a chance at life and he knows it. He's grateful."

"I don't want his gratitude!" Amanda was torn by conflicting emotions. "I'm his mother, I want his love!"

Garth understood the feelings behind Amanda's uncharacteristic outburst, though he wrestled with the concept and meaning of love daily. He wished he could tell her that Jason wanted her for a mother as badly as she wanted to be able to be his mother. But it wouldn't be fair. Because Jason wanted her to be more than his mother. He wanted them to be a family. Besides the fact that they'd really just met, Garth never intended to have another wife.

Karen had cured him of marriage for good. He was not foolish enough to believe he'd caused Karen's problems but he knew he hadn't handled them right, either. Her stealing of Jason and her subsequent suicide were ample proof of his failure. There were no happily-ever-afters for some people. And he was one of those people.

"It'll take time. For your sake, I wish we could walk in there right now and tell him the whole story. But we can't. Just be there when he needs you,

Amanda, and pretty soon his gratitude will turn to something more. Then he'll turn to you.''

Garth watched the internal struggle going on inside Amanda as it reflected on her face. She'd been robbed of so much and he knew from the look on her face when he'd glanced up to see her standing in Jason's doorway that she blamed him.

She wasn't alone. He blamed himself. He hadn't recognized Karen's illness until it was too late. He'd been so wrapped up in his career and what he wanted from marriage that he'd fooled himself into believing that Karen was just spoiled and demanding. He hadn't even considered that she might be mentally ill. By the time he recognized her actions as an illness it was too late. He'd already called it quits in New Orleans. And when he'd cut her loose, she'd apparently turned around and come up with an insanely brilliant scheme to steal her way back into his good graces. She'd stolen Jason from Amanda. The damage was done. And he'd become a father.

For a while, anyway.

Garth ran through the parking garage and into the hospital, not caring if anyone stared at him. Jason was in trouble. Damn! He'd been doing so well. After that initial bad bout, the antinausea drug had taken hold. Then two hours ago, Garth's mother had called but he'd been deep in negotiations on a new contract. The secretary of the man he'd been meeting with hadn't understood the nature of the call. He'd been angry but had masked that anger because he needed the business her boss's company would provide.

When he'd left, he'd broken every speed limit on the expressway.

Would that elevator never come? he thought as he jabbed the button repeatedly. Garth ran through the conversation he'd had with his mother for the hundredth time since jamming his key in the ignition and peeling out of his parking spot.

Jason had become hysterical over something he'd seen on television. Frieda Jorgensen had promised to do whatever was necessary to calm him but she wanted Garth and Amanda to hurry right over. Garth had hoped he'd be able to calm Jason down before Amanda saw him since she'd only be able to enter his room as a new friend. Unfortunately by now, Amanda had probably gotten there before him and had been forced to stand by and watch her own son being comforted by another. And there was always the possibility that Jason would lash out at her because he thought she was a hospital employee.

The past year hadn't been without incidents like this. Even the mildest mannered kid acted out once in a while when practically every adult he saw came into his life to inflict one kind of pain or another. Even volunteers who only played games with him to help occupy his time had been targets at those times. He could only hope Amanda's reception hadn't been too bad.

What had Garth so worried this time was that his mother's tone had sounded different from those other times. As if something had shaken Jason badly. Garth checked his watch. Where was that elevator? And what had set Jason off?

Garth heard the frantic click of high heels on terrazzo. He turned and saw Amanda racing toward the elevators from across the lobby. She looked as frantic as he felt but he hid his worry. Too many times since meeting Amanda, she had needed to shore up his faltering strength. Now, from somewhere deep inside he had to do the same for her.

At that moment the elevator finally came. Garth stepped inside and held the doors open for Amanda. He quickly stepped backward as Amanda rushed inside. "Garth," she gasped as the doors slid shut behind them. She stayed facing him and sagged, clearly exhausted, against the closed elevator doors. "How is he? What happened? I decided to take a cab but it got caught in a huge traffic jam on the Schuylkill. I'm so sorry it took me so long."

Garth shrugged trying to look nonchalant and not give away his roiling emotions. "Don't worry about it. I just got here myself. I was in a meeting and didn't get the message. As for Jason, I'm sure it isn't anything to be too frantic about. He's gotten upset before over tests and whatnot. Sometimes he just can't take any more poking and prodding. Mother did say though that this time it was a television show that upset him."

"What could he have seen on television?"

Garth leaned his back against the wall and jammed his hands into his pockets to keep from pulling her into his arms and comforting her. "Maybe he saw something negative about bone marrow transplants. I don't know." All Garth really knew at this point was that his mom had sounded frantic and nothing shook his mother.

Matt Hernandez met them outside Jason's room.

His words were quick and concise, his manner grave. "I don't care what you have to say or do. Calm him any way you can. It's imperative that you reassure him."

Reluctant yet impatient, Garth pushed open the door to Jason's room without any response to Hernandez. Jason lay in the bed looking smaller and more forlorn than Garth had ever seen him. His big violet eyes, the only trait he seemed to have gotten from his mother, were red rimmed and swollen. Worse there was a panic in them he'd never seen before. Even the day he'd heard that leukemia could be fatal. "Hey, kiddo, what's the trouble?"

Jason looked up as a tear rolled out of the corner of his eye and into his ear. "You lied to me," he said in a barely audible whisper.

Garth frowned and leaned closer. "Son, I've never lied to you."

"Yes, you did. I'm not your son."

Garth felt a knife thrust through his heart as his blood drained into his toes. For a moment he couldn't breathe. "Jason, where did you hear something like that?"

"The man on 'The Nick Terry Show.' He said I don't belong to you. He said I'd have to go live with Mrs. Powers. He said she was my mother and that my…moth…your…your wife…stole me when I was a baby. Why, Daddy? Why did you lie to me?"

Looking into the devastated eyes of his son, Garth knew the full depth of the heartbreak he'd already been feeling for weeks. "I didn't lie, Jason. You look just like me and I didn't know what she'd done. She'd been gone awhile and when I saw you, I accepted what she said. You were my son from the moment I saw you."

Jason's bottom lip quivered. "I'm so much trouble and all and I'm not yours anyway. I guess you don't want me anymore."

Garth stared at Jason, staggered. "Jason, that's not true! I'll always want you and think of you as my son but you see...Amanda...is—"

Garth's mother stomped on his foot. Hard. "For goodness sake, Garth. Stop pussyfooting around. Can't you see that Jason's upset and worried about how all this will affect him? You can't keep your plans a secret any longer, thanks to some wretched person who blabbed the whole story to that tacky, morning talk show.

"Jason, lamb." Frieda took a deep breath. "What your father has been trying to keep as a surprise is that he and Amanda have decided that the best solution for all of us is to be a family. They're getting married. Garth will still be your father and you'll have Amanda for a mother."

Garth stared at his mother. Was she out of her mind? The silence in the room seemed answer enough. One glance at Amanda told him she was as appalled as he was by the whopper his mother had told. Did she really think a savvy kid like Jason was going to swallow a tall tale like that?

"Really?" Jason asked, hope a living thing in his voice. Garth stared down at Jason—a different Jason, a changed Jason, a happy, beaming Jason. "You still want to be my father and Mrs. Powers is really my mother? She's going to live with us? For real?"

Garth turned toward Amanda again. He bristled.

She was as white as Jason's sheets. Okay. His mother had dropped a real bomb here. He wanted to give her a piece of his mind, too, but did Amanda have to look so…so horrified? He might not be a movie star but he wasn't some monster. And his house might not be the governor's mansion but it was a pretty terrific house, second mortgage and all. He didn't share her faith, but he wasn't a bad person. Did she have to look as if marriage to him would be a fate worse than death?

What was he thinking? Of course it was! For him, too. He didn't want a wife. Especially not one who looked so horrified at the prospect of having him for a husband. He glanced back at Jason, who had begun to look worried again, and leapt from the frying pan into the fire. Jason was all that mattered. He'd walk through fire to save him.

Garth took two long steps, which put him next to Amanda. She still stood barely inside the room. He smiled and, putting an arm around her, pulled her to the bed to stand with him beside Jason. "Since your grandmother let the cat out of the bag, son, I guess it's time we shared our plans with you. Right, sweetheart?" Garth said and squeezed Amanda's shoulder.

"Absolutely," Amanda answered. Her mind in a whirl, she forced a smile in Jason's direction then looked at Garth. He looked…stunned when she wrapped her arm around his waist. Good! Two could play at this game. Whatever the game was.

"And you're really my real mom?" Jason asked. "And you looked for me for years and years until you found me?"

Amanda nodded. "I looked for years and years but

actually, it was your father who found me," Amanda corrected. She was annoyed at Garth but she had to give Garth his due. "He found out that his wife had kidnapped you. So he looked for me. He made me so happy. It was like a dream come true when he told me where you were."

Jason pushed himself up in the bed. It was the most strength and determination he'd displayed in days. "He was your Prince Charming," Jason said dreamily. "He rescued you and you fell in love. Right?"

Amanda felt like Alice just after she'd blundered down the rabbit hole. How could the child who'd rationally discussed heaven and death with her and who beat her twice a day at Monopoly believe in fairy tales? "That's not—" Amanda broke off when Garth squeezed her arm.

"That's about the size of it," Garth put in.

"Do I call you Mom?" Jason asked.

"You can call me whatever you feel comfortable with."

"Mom, I think." Jason stared off into space for a few minutes. "What do you want to call me?" he wondered. "Is Jason my real name, Mom?"

Amanda had never heard so wonderful a sound as "Mom" on her son's lips. She had waited so long. *Mom.* Her heart swelled with mingled pain and joy. "I named you Jesse but I don't expect you to use that name unless it's what you want. You're Jason now. That's even how I think of you."

Jason looked ponderous. "It's my real father's name, isn't it?"

"You were named for your father. He died before you were born."

"He died because he was a hero like Dad!" Jason frowned. "I remember what you told me about your husband. When he tried to save a lady in a holdup, he got shot."

Amanda nodded as she vowed to remember what Jason had innocently reminded her of. Garth and Jess certainly were two of a kind. And, because of that, she had to find a way to undo the damage Frieda and Garth had done with this engagement story. True, they could make it a long engagement, using Jason's health as an excuse and never marry, but the pretense would put them in contact with each other too much.

"Mom," Jason said as if from a distance. "Isn't that a good idea?"

Amanda had no idea what he'd said but she decided a noncommittal answer was better than letting him know how distracted and upset she was. "I suppose," she said.

She was surprised when Garth glared at her. "Son, I'm not sure. You're going into isolation any day. That's short notice and your doctors might not let you come anyway. I think we'd better wait until you're at home and on the road to recovery."

"But that could be months! I want you to get married now. Why does everything have to get ruined because I'm sick? If I were dead, you two could be happy and have other kids. You wouldn't have to waste all your time here with me."

"Jason! Don't talk that way! It isn't true," Garth said. "The time we spend with you is precious. Besides that, it was you who brought Amanda and me together. You're an important part of our lives. Nothing would be the same without you."

Jason brightened. "Then you'll get married in the hospital chapel and get them to let me go. I want us to be a family right away!"

Amanda held her breath. Garth would think of something. She'd seen how fast he was when dealing with Jason's machinations. Her heart stopped when he nodded in defeat. "I'll see what I can do."

"Well now," Frieda said with a smile worthy only of a cat with canary indigestion. "If there's going to be a wedding, you and Amanda better not waste a minute. I'll stay with Jason this evening and you two can go see Reverend Pittman. I'll call him and smooth the way. I'm sure he'll be delighted to perform the ceremony here. And I'm sure you've got a great deal to discuss between you."

"But I'd like a word with you, Mother," Garth said, his teeth gritted in a semblance of a smile.

Frieda waved aside Garth's reasonable request. "You don't need me to plan your wedding. Run along, children. I'll see you both at home after visiting hours."

Amanda followed Garth out of the room after kissing Jason on the forehead. "Why did you agree?" Garth snarled as soon as the door closed on Jason and Frieda.

"Me!" Amanda squeaked. "It was you who acted as if we'd planned it all along. I was so shocked that I answered a question I didn't even hear. It was your mother who trapped us. How could she do this?"

"You saw how upset he was. He calmed down

right away when she said we'd be a family. What else could she have said?''

Since Amanda didn't have a better answer, she asked another burning question. ''What are we going to do?''

Garth's jaw hardened with determination. ''We're going to get married.''

Chapter Five

Amanda gaped at Garth. "Are you out of your mind? I refuse to even consider marrying you!"

Garth's eyes suddenly blazed. "You wanted Jason to know you're his mother and now that's happened. What are you going to do with that privilege? Walk in there and burst his bubble?"

Amanda's temper flared, too. "Your mother shouldn't have created the *bubble* in the first place!"

"Look, Amanda." Garth inhaled deeply and let his breath ease out. "This is about more than just my mother's...story. The bubble I'm talking about is his security and I've been that security for as long as Jason remembers."

"I'm not debating that, but I would have been there for him if I could have. If I'd been allowed to."

"And I'm not debating that. And for the record it was Karen's fault that you weren't a mother to Jason all those years. Not mine," Garth continued. "I can't tell you how sorry I am that all this happened. I even feel partly responsible. She may have hoped to hold on to me through the baby. But guilt aside, I also know Jason can't lose me right now. The connection forged between us in the past seven years can't be wiped out by your arrival on the scene and your rights to him. I thought for a while it could, but hearing his take on this made me realize that I was wrong. I hadn't thought he'd feel deserted or that he'd been too much trouble. I wish it didn't have to be this way but that's the way it is.''

"You don't want to marry me any more than I want to marry you. That's what you're saying."

Garth nodded. "That's what I'm saying. But I'm willing to put aside my feelings for Jason's best interests."

"I hardly even know you!" Amanda railed. "And this is about more than feelings."

Garth shrugged. "It doesn't have to be a real marriage and we can end it when Jason's health is secure."

Amanda turned away and walked into the nearby solarium. She stared out over the city and wondered if anyone else in that sea of humanity faced so monumental a decision that day. No, she corrected herself, there really wasn't a decision and that was the problem. She'd been forced into a corner by a gossip and a desperate grandmother.

But more was at stake here than Jason's health and peace of mind. She had to wonder if Garth saw this marriage as a way to increase his legal chances to stay a part of Jason's life. And what of her vow never again to become unequally yoked to an unbelieving partner in marriage. This marriage, that he seemed all too willing to toss aside when it no longer suited his purposes, for her would be a lifetime commitment no matter what an earthly court decreed. She could never stand before a minister of the Lord and vow her life to Garth with an option-out clause in the marriage contract tucked in the back of her mind.

It was all too much. Here she was still trying to cope with finding Jason and discovering him ill—now it looked as if she was trapped into a sham of a marriage with a man she feared she could easily love. No matter what, Amanda knew she was bound to be hurt. Because if she agreed, it would be her duty to try to make their marriage work. And if she took that course, how could she possibly guard her heart in case he did toss her aside as soon as Jason was well? Amanda wondered if she even had a right to try protecting herself when that would mean giving less than her all to her marriage.

Her only choice seemed to be to agree and pray that Garth would see how rewarding marriage could be. She'd be a good wife to him and hope he would begin to feel for her some of what she had begun to feel for him. She'd also use any opportunities presented to her to show him the kind of peace and joy putting the Lord back in his life could bring.

Amanda turned from the sight of the towering city to face Garth. She leaned against the windowsill and crossed her arms. "I need to pray about this, Garth. It's a big step."

Garth's eyes went as hard as diamonds. "I don't see what you need to *pray* about. Jason's life or your temporary inconvenience. It won't be all that long. I want out of this marriage as much as you do.''

Amanda fought the urge to flinch. Why did he react so badly to any mention of her faith and how could he look on a vow made to God as inconsequential? "Exactly how long do you intend for us to stay married?" she asked tightly.

"Until Jason is stronger and has adjusted to our new roles in his life. Then we can separate amicably.''

"Amicably?" she repeated, but the question in her voice told of her doubts. "And what about Jason at that point? Where does he fit into the *amicable* divorce?"

"All I ask is that you let me see him. As I said, you were right about that. I can't just drop out of his life. After the way he talked just now, I'm afraid he'd think I don't care about him. I want him to always be able to trust in my feelings for him even though I'm not his real father.''

Amanda's anger drained. Garth once again seemed to be thinking of her son first. But the loss of her anger left a void and a question that had been nagging at the back of her mind. Why did Garth, who obviously loved Jason with every fiber of his being, never say the words? To Jason or anyone else for that matter. She shook her head clearing away the deep questions that kept gnawing away at her. It was the practical she had to deal with just then. "Garth, you are his father but I still want an agreement worked out up front. I'd be eroding my right to sole custody with a marriage to you. I can't risk losing him again. I don't even have any guarantee that it wasn't you who leaked our story to that show. Maybe you and your mother thought keeping a legal foot in the door was worth the gamble with Jason's health.''

Garth's jaw hardened even more. His eyes glittered and she could almost see steam come out his ears. Amanda was ashamed. For a second she'd considered the possibility of a conspiracy between Garth and Frieda Jorgensen but had dismissed it the next. These people loved her son, so why had she said that? Just because the word seemed to be missing from his vocabulary?

''Garth, I—''

''What happened to all that trust you talked about yesterday?'' he asked through gritted teeth.

Amanda wished his anger didn't make her feel so awful. It meant she cared and that almost guaranteed she'd be hurt badly eventually. ''I'm sorry. I guess it went out the window with my sense. I shouldn't have said that. I shouldn't even have thought it. I'm afraid, Garth. Can you understand that?''

Garth stared at her with a hard uncompromising look in his eyes. ''Don't worry, you'll get your agreement. And while we're on the subject, I have a demand of my own. I want a prenuptial agreement stating that you have no claim on Liberty Express or the house.''

Amanda was once again surprised at the way Garth's cold anger affected her. She felt like crying. ''Fine.'' She forced the word past nearly trembling lips and turned away. ''Just give me a few minutes in the chapel and I'll have my answer.''

Dear God, is it already too late? Do I already care too much? Amanda asked silently as she walked toward the chapel. She entered, her mind in a whirl, fears overwhelming her. *Why did I even hesitate? What choice do I have?* She looked around, peace an impossible commodity, the voice of her Lord silent in the face of thundering anxieties. Amanda turned and left. Garth had been right. What was there to pray about? She had no choice.

Amanda stared at the woman in the mirror. The ivory lace, tea-length dress was something out of her fantasies. How had she wound up dressed like this in the middle of her worst nightmare? Ah yes, Amanda thought, that first run-in with my would-be mother-in-law's iron will....

"Amanda you can't wear that to your wedding!" Frieda exclaimed in horror as they left the hospital.

Amanda sighed, gazing down at her blue-flowered dress. "Why can't I wear this? It's perfectly presentable."

"Tomorrow you'll be a bride and you can't wear a dress you wear all the time no matter how nice it is. Garth's seen you in that more than once."

"I didn't have time to plan my trip north. I just threw some things in a bag."

"It isn't that he's seen you in it," Frieda explained, slowly as if Amanda were missing some or most of her marbles. "This should be a special occasion. A celebration!"

"Then why do I feel as if I'm a lamb being led to slaughter?" Amanda hated the sullen tone in her voice.

"How long are you going to keep this up?" Frieda snapped.

"Keep what up?"

The older woman took Amanda's arm and pointed her toward the curb and the taxi stand. "How long are you going to keep up the pretense that you aren't attracted to my son? Amanda, I've seen the way you look at Garth. He's quite a catch, if I do say so myself."

"Garth is a very nice man," Amanda hedged as she climbed into the taxi. "But so was my husband."

"Nice, but he's not what you need?"

Amanda nodded.

"And your late husband was a believer. Is that it?"

Amanda bit her lip. She just couldn't lie to this woman who'd helped raise her son. "It isn't my place to judge Garth or Jess. Let's just say Jess wasn't a committed Christian. I thought it wouldn't matter. After we moved to the city, Jess changed. He cared about other things besides our marriage and the family we'd planned."

"And those things hurt you?"

"No. Those things were more important than me. And as for being attracted to Garth, I was as attracted to Jess. *Attraction* is another word for *temptation* as far as I'm concerned. My old pastor used to say that temptation doesn't happen with things that are good for us."

Frieda sighed and closed her eyes. "Oh, Amanda, I can't believe I got you into this. I knew in my heart it wasn't fair to you but I love my son. I confess I've seen you as a sort of godsend for Garth. I hoped that through your example he'd see how wrong he is for not trusting in the Lord. He just can't keep on carrying the burden he has in these years alone. He needs to rely on the Lord. He needs His strength. His comfort.''

Amanda shrugged. ''Don't count too much on me to help bring him to the Lord. I doubt he'll be looking at me as any great example. I'm going to try, but you have to realize that Garth sees both of us as fools who believe in fairy tales. Besides, according to Garth this marriage is only a temporary arrangement.''

Frieda balled her fist in her lap, deep disappointment evident on her face. ''I could shake that boy for turning his back on everything he once believed in.''

''Once believed?''

''As a boy, he loved the Lord so much. I thought...'' Frieda trailed off, her eyes filling.

Amanda reached out and grasped Frieda's hand. ''What is it? What did you think? What happened?''

''It isn't all my own story to tell. Actually, my part of it was settled a long time ago. But what turned Garth against the Lord is another story in a way. It's how my problems affected him so it's his story now. I think you should ask him. I don't want him thinking I've been interfering more than I already have.''

''Would you answer one question for me?''

''If I can, dear.''

''I've noticed that Garth never says the word *love*.

Even to Jason. It could be that I'm imagining it but—''

''You aren't imagining a thing. No, he doesn't acknowledge love any more than he does the Lord. And before you ask, it is because of the same thing. Ask him if the opportunity presents itself. Right now I have a question for you. Does Garth understand that you'll consider yours a marriage for life?''

''No. And I have to ask you not to tell him anything about this conversation. If he stays with me, it has to be of his own free will, just as if he turns to the Lord, it has to come from his heart. Not his lips. I need you to understand that I could very easily love Garth more than I ever did Jess. I know that already. But if Garth can marry and plan to end that marriage so easily, then I can't trust him with my heart.''

Frieda pursed her lips and set her shoulders. ''I understand completely but you still have to look the part for Jason. Suppose we stop on the way home. I know a lovely little dress shop in Haverford. They're sure to be able—''

Tempted, Amanda interrupted before she could weaken. ''No, I—I can't.''

''Why?''

''It wouldn't be wise.''

Frieda batted her hand at the air in front of her. ''Oh, fiddle with being wise. Neither you nor Garth seem to think this marriage is going to last, but I believe this was meant to be. If it does turn into something wonderful and lasting, would you want to look back on tomorrow and remember yourself in your blue-flowered dress?''

"It isn't exactly a rag," Amanda hedged, refusing to let herself hope that there could be a happily-ever-after for her and Garth.

"It just won't do!" Frieda reiterated, losing her patience. "Jason will think it's strange for you to wear a dress he's already seen. It will upset him. He's already asked if your dress has pearls and a train."

"I don't think—"

"That's right! You've got it. Don't think. Driver..."

And that's why I'm wearing this beautiful dress, Amanda thought as she stood in a room across the hall from the chapel of Children's Hospital in Philadelphia. She fingered her dress, the most beautiful, expensive, over-thirty wedding dress the Lysette Shop could furnish.

She'd meant to hate everything the proprietor showed her and had done herself proud until the sneaky woman had brought out and installed Amanda in the dress she now wore. Frieda had seen something Amanda couldn't hide and had declared the dress sold and her wedding gift to Amanda. The price tag had horrified Amanda but Frieda had waved away any protests. Matching pearl combs and a pair of lacy pumps were soon added to the growing pile on the counter.

Amanda grumbled, "I feel like a Thanksgiving turkey. All trussed up, dressed up and ready for sacrifice."

"Well, you look absolutely beautiful," Frieda said

from behind her as she fussed with the combs in Amanda's hair. Frieda had insisted that Amanda apply what she called "full party makeup" as well. So she looked in the mirror and saw eyes that looked even larger than usual. Amanda hoped Jason wouldn't be able to see past the eyeliner, blush and lipstick to the fearful woman beneath.

"Thanks to you. I don't think anyone back home would recognize me. I doubt Garth and Jason will, either."

Christina Jorgensen, Garth's sister and Amanda's maid of honor, laughed. "Garth is in for a surprise. That's for sure."

Amanda fiddled with the engagement ring Garth had given her and insisted she wear. It was for appearance's sake only, he'd assured her. "I'm not sure I can do this," she admitted.

Christina took hold of Amanda's cold hand and squeezed gently. "Of course, you can. I'll be right there by your side. It's a maid of honor's job to help out the bride."

"And if you get tongue-tied, I'll just shout out the I do's for you," Frieda teased.

Amanda smiled but she wasn't at all sure if the older Jorgensen woman had made a promise or a threat. She looked up into Frieda's smiling face and detected nothing but support. But still, she wondered. "This really isn't what Garth wanted, either," Amanda said.

Frieda raised an eyebrow. "Is that what you think? Let me tell you, nothing and no one has ever made my son do something he didn't want to do."

"You can say that again," Christina agreed.

Amanda allowed a small hope to spark in her soul.

"And on that subject, Garth asked me to give you these. This is your wedding gift," his mother said.

Amanda stared at the flat jeweler's box Frieda had placed in her hands.

"Open it," Christina demanded.

What looked like an antique seed pearl choker and matching earrings lay on a bed of age-yellowed satin. "Oh, my goodness!" Amanda's eyes flew to Frieda's then Christina's.

"Grandmother's wedding jewelry," Garth's sister said.

The spark of hope flared in Amanda's heart. Why would he give her these if he meant to end the marriage? "But, why would he do this? I can't accept these under false pretenses."

"Oh, yes you can!" Frieda exclaimed. "Those will be Jason's one day to give his wife. It's a tradition. One I'd thought Garth had forgotten. It's a good sign. Now, let's get those on you."

"Who knows how long this marriage'll last?" her smug maid of honor added cryptically as she handed Amanda a small cascade of gardenias and baby's breath while her new mother-in-law finished with the clasp. "These are from him, too. He said he remembered you grew them."

Amanda felt her eyes fill. "Why did he have to make such sweet gestures?" She bent her head to smell the heady sweetness of her flowers.

Frieda chuckled. "Oh, you've got lots of surprises

ahead of you being married to my son. He is, after all, *my* son."

There was a knock on the door. "Everything's ready," a voice called from the hall.

"Here we go," Frieda said cheerfully. "Curtain's going up."

Amanda swallowed. It was curtains for her. That was for sure! *Oh, help me Lord!*

Chapter Six

~~~~

For Amanda, the short walk across the hall to the chapel was sheer torture. There weren't just a few butterflies ricocheting around in her stomach. This was more like a whole flock of sparrows.

Her steps faltered on the threshold as a nurse began to play the wedding march on an acoustic guitar. Amanda looked around at the curious staff who'd squeezed into the tiny chapel next to several of Garth's employees and a handful of his family and friends. It struck Amanda that she'd never felt so alone in her life, not even standing at her husband's graveside amid scores of consoling strangers who hadn't a clue about her real feelings.

She sought out Jason with desperate eyes and found him sitting on a high stool at the foot of the plain altar between Dr. Bill Wood, Garth's best man, and Christina. Jason looked frail and tired but his eyes shone with delight and excitement. She glanced at the pillow in his lap. He had his own special part in the ceremony. Since he was too weak to walk up the aisle, Garth had dubbed him the official ring *keeper*. Amanda looked at her son's face again. It was his look of hope that gave her the courage to step fully inside the chapel.

But fear and isolation surrounded her. Jason was the only one in the room who was there for her and even *his* affections were divided. Jason glanced back at the cross over the altar and Amanda remembered that she was never alone. Then a deeper realization dawned. Her Lord would have to protect her from hurt because deep in her heart, Amanda knew her fear sprang from a foolish, dangerous wish that Garth wanted this marriage because of her as much as because of Jason.

Garth startled her when he stepped to her side even though the plan had been to meet her at the altar. Amanda looked up and saw sympathy and understanding in his compelling gaze. He took her trembling hand and tucked it around his arm, covering her hand with his. Any remnant of loneliness fled.

"It's going to be okay," he whispered.

Amanda smiled up at him tentatively and Garth felt his heart catch. She was a lovely, brave and incredibly noble woman. What man wouldn't want her for his wife? He thought she deserved so much more than a man like him who'd failed so miserably at his first marriage. He hated failure. In fact, thanks to his father's constant haranguing, he feared it. That was why his total failure with Karen had hurt so much.

He wondered suddenly how all this had come about. Could his mother be right about lives being directed by God? Could He really have used

Amanda's tragic loss of her son and his own near loss of that same child for good? How else had he wound up marrying someone who deserved so much better than him? Garth couldn't smother the sudden wish that his mother was right about a lot of things, especially that someday he and Amanda would look back on this forced wedding as a miracle.

Jason beamed at them when they drew even with him. The next minutes seemed to speed by so fast that Garth found himself doing as he was told without thought. The minister began the traditional words of the ceremony. His sister, Chris, acting as Amanda's maid of honor, took her bouquet as Jason handed the rings over. Amanda repeated the same empty promises he had but with such a ring of truth to them that he found himself wishing she really did mean them.

Then it was over. In the eyes of everyone there, he had just taken a wife. Garth looked from Amanda to his mother and sister, then glanced up at the ceiling toward the heavens. Had he taken a wife before Him as well?

Garth once again obeyed a voice on the periphery of his thoughts and leaned down to drop a simple peck on Amanda's cheek. But she turned her head just then and their lips met. Met and clung for two, then three lingering seconds before he somehow marshaled the willpower to step away.

They stared at each other.

"Where are you taking Mom for your honeymoon?" Jason asked into the ensuing silence. Garth looked away from Amanda and forced a laugh. He turned and scooped Jason into his arms then settled him in a wheelchair. "Somewhere you're not, kiddo," Garth told Jason as he tugged on the peak of his ever-present Phillies cap. Garth's quip drew a laugh from everyone but Amanda.

"I'll push Jason back, Garth," Chris said. "You should escort your new wife upstairs. Wait a few minutes though, Jason has a surprise planned in his room," she added in a whisper.

Amanda grabbed his sleeve and Garth turned back to face her as his sister pushed Jason toward the door. He was surprised to see near panic in Amanda's eyes. "We can't leave the city. He needs us. I can't go. Not now. I just can't. You have to think of an excuse. I'd feel as if I'm deserting him."

"Are you implying I wouldn't?" Garth growled. All traces of the strange, altered state of reality into which he'd fallen during the ceremony fled. How could he have forgotten the way she'd fought this marriage or the low opinion she had of him?

Amanda put her hand to her head, then looked back up at him. "No. Of course not." Garth noticed tears well up in Amanda's violet eyes, seeming to drown their vibrant color in sorrow. "I just can't go away," she continued needlessly. "Just going home at night hurts."

Garth's anger melted, though her revulsion over having to marry him still stung. "Amanda, I was only trying to break the ice and pass off Jason's question without a real answer. I have no intention of taking you anywhere but home. It was a joke."

"Oh. I...I guess I overreacted. I'm sorry, Garth. I should have realized that."

"It's okay. I'm sorry, too. It was probably a bad

joke." Garth took Amanda's arm and directed her toward the door.

Amanda smiled up at him, violets seeming to sparkle in her still moist eyes. "If Jason weren't sick, it would have been funny. Really," she assured him. "I should have recognized that kind of male humor. It's something Jess would have said. Cops are notoriously irreverent."

Garth stiffened at the reference to her former husband. Before he recognized his own jealousy he said, "Pilots aren't that different from cops. We both wear uniforms and some of us never come home from work again, either. Who knows, maybe I'll go down in flames one of these fine days and you'll be rid of me."

Amanda felt the blood drain from her face and she quickly looked away. How could he think she'd wish him harm? Had she somehow given him the impression that she did? True, she didn't trust him. She was afraid to, because she knew he couldn't wait for the day Jason was healthy so he could divorce her. Her lack of trust was only because it would be so easy to love the man. Certainly not because she hated him!

Just then Amanda noticed Bill Wood's head peek out the door to Jason's room as she and Garth approached and she lost her opportunity to contradict his assumption. In a voice that sounded like a caricature of a wedding palace master of ceremonies, Bill said, "And now, ladies and gentlemen, for the first time ever, may I present Mr. and Mrs. Garth Jorgensen."

They walked in and found Frieda, Christina, Bill Wood, Dr. Matt Hernandez and his sister who'd played in the chapel. There was a cake on Jason's bed table.

"My goodness. Who arranged all this?" Amanda gasped.

"I did!" Jason beamed. "Me and Doc Wood. But you guys got to cut the cake and give it out, then toss your bouquet real fast, Mom. That way my nurses can go and we won't have so many people in here." Conspiratorially, in a stage whisper Jason said, "We don't want to get Doctor Matt or Doc Wood in trouble with their bosses."

Amanda laughed and she and Garth made short work of the cake. She hated to toss her flowers away but knew it was foolish to feel sentimental about them even if they had come from the most wonderful man she'd ever met. Jason's nurses left after one of them caught her bouquet.

Amanda felt a tap on her shoulder as Maria Hernandez, Matt's sister, began to play a slow tune. "I think this is our dance, Mrs. Jorgensen," Garth said.

Turning into his arms, Amanda tried to ignore the song's promises. They would not grow old together. There was nothing in their future but the ending that had begun the day they'd met. Amanda blinked away the hot tears that burned at the back of her throat. *I think I've made a big mistake, Jesus. I'm sorry I didn't take the time to listen to your advice.*

Amanda gave up trying to get back to sleep. It was nearly dawn anyway. Thankfully the sun would soon chase away the night. Her wedding night. She shook her head ruefully. Hers had certainly been an unconventional one.

She glanced around her room and remembered her surprise when Garth had gathered her in his arms at the front door. But fairy tales were for children. He'd deposited her in the front hall, turned and walked back out of the house. She'd heard him return hours later, sometime after two.

Amanda watched as the sun rose, its light filtering through the bare but majestic trees that surrounded Garth's house. Garth's house. Jason's house. Even Frieda called it home. But it wasn't Amanda's home and it never would be. She'd given up any right to it without even a thought.

Now that all was said and done, she realized that she should probably have found a lawyer to represent her interests. She'd signed both the prenuptial agreement Garth had wanted and the custody agreement she'd demanded, reading only the latter.

When Jason was well enough and they divorced, Garth would have Jason with him every other weekend, one month of the summer and on alternating holidays excluding Christmas. That had been the one item she'd had an objection to. She wanted Jason's Christmases for the next seven years. She'd already missed six of them, she'd told Garth, and he'd acquiesced immediately, grateful that she'd planned to allow him as much time as she did. Amanda had dismissed his thanks. The arrangements were for Jason, not Garth, she'd told him, trying to remain detached.

As for the financial agreement that included the house, Amanda hadn't even thought to read it. Garth owned nothing she wanted.

"Amanda?"

She pivoted toward the door. "Come in," she called. Garth pushed the door open but stood in the hall wearing a robe with a towel hooked around his neck. "If you want a ride into the city, I'll be ready to leave in about an hour."

"But, Garth, that's an awful lot of trouble. I can take the train," she told him needing a bit of distance after the soul-searching minutes she'd just spent. "Taking me to the hospital's too far out of your way."

"It's no trouble. All I'll do is get off the expressway, drop you off and get back on at the next exit." He glanced at the window. "It looks like rain. You'd have to take a cab from the train. Come on. Shake a leg."

"You shake me up enough already," she muttered.

"Did you say something?" Garth asked then chuckled.

Amanda scowled, wondering what he'd heard. "And just what do you find so funny?" she asked as he turned and sauntered down the hall.

Two hours later, Amanda managed to keep herself from bolting from the car before Garth pulled to a complete standstill. She did open the door as soon as the car rolled to a stop but Garth reached out before she got her seat belt off. He brushed her hair off her shoulder. She froze at the feel of his fingers brushing her neck.

"Amanda," he whispered. "You've scarcely said a word all the way in. Don't I even get a thank-you for driving you?"

Appalled by her lack of manners, Amanda turned her head to apologize and thank him. But Garth wanted more than words. His lips settled over hers.

Amanda forgot fears and worries. She forgot the rest of the world.

Beep! Beep! Beep! "Hey, Mack, kiss the old lady at home will ya? I got a fare to pick up!"

Amanda jerked back. Garth glared out the back window at the taxi behind him, then looked back at the passenger seat. Amanda had slipped away in the blink on an eye. He smiled as he watched her disappear through the large glass doors into the hospital lobby. The cabby beeped again and Garth waved off his complaints as he faced front and pulled away from the curb.

The kiss confirmed Garth's suspicions. Yesterday when they'd gone to Jason's room for the wedding reception, Amanda had stayed as far from him as possible while going through all the motions expected of her. He'd been a bit insulted but he couldn't resist having her near when Maria had played that song. The dance had been a spur-of-the-moment decision but it had been an eye-opener.

Amanda wasn't as against this marriage as she'd seemed. When he'd demanded the dance, she'd melted as if as powerless to resist him as he was to resist her. But there was more than physical desire at work on his side. This wasn't just the lust Karen had once inspired.

He'd never missed Karen the way he did Amanda and that was after knowing her such a short while. He'd see something and think, I wish Amanda had seen that. Or he'd hear a news story and wonder what

Amanda would think of it. Jason would say something delightful and he'd wish she were there to share the moment. Now that his pride wasn't so sore, he wondered if he wasn't falling in love with her.

Love.

Until Amanda had come into his life he been unable to even think the word. Now more and more it and its meaning floated through his head at the oddest times.

But even if he did love her it didn't matter. He couldn't let it. He didn't have the right to hold Amanda in a marriage with a man she didn't love and who she'd been trapped into marrying.

That was the question that had sent him out of the house on his wedding night. He knew it had been wrong to dump Amanda in the foyer without so much as a goodbye. But after that dance and then having given in to the romantic gesture of carrying her over the threshold, he'd had no choice. One word and he'd have been begging her to let him make their marriage real. And that wouldn't have been fair.

Garth wound his way through traffic and arrived at the hangar without the slightest idea what the answer to his dilemma was or what to do next. Sometimes he wished he had a father to turn to but then he never had. Love hadn't mattered when he'd needed it most.

In the back corner of his mind a voice whispered that he always had and still did have a Father. A Father who would not fail him as his mortal father had. He stubbornly silenced the voice.

"So, Matt Hernandez thinks they'll do the transplant at the end of next week?" Garth asked Amanda as they made their way toward the parking garage. They'd been married a week and had fallen into a routine. Unfortunately, the routine kept them apart for all but an hour a day. She'd hoped for more time to show him how good marriage could be.

"He thinks from the way the tests look that Jason will be ready sooner than he thought."

"That's a break." Garth's voice broke and he stopped walking. He took a fortifying breath. "I can't stand this. He looks worse now than he ever has." Garth grimaced and raked a hand through his hair. "I'm sorry. I keep falling apart on you."

Amanda noticed a small sitting area to their left. She took his arm and motioned toward the seats. "You're entitled to lean on someone, Garth," she told him as she sat next to him. "It's been a long year for you. I don't know how you do it alone."

"Well, it's been a tough seven for you and you haven't fallen apart," he replied.

"Garth, first off, that was not falling apart." She gave him what she hoped was a reassuring smile. "But as far as how I survive, I've told you. Jesus takes care of the worry and gives me peace. I still have to handle everything that comes along but He's there for me to lean on. If you'd ask Him for help, He'd be there to hold you up, too. Believe me."

"Maybe I don't want *His* help," he snapped. "What kind of a God lets anyone, let alone a child, go through the torture Jason has? What kind of God deserts a kid who believes in him?"

Amanda knew an opportunity when she saw it. She'd bided her time and now it was here. "De-

serted? Garth, take off the blinders. Look at Jason.
Does he look deserted to you? Ask him what his faith
gives him. It isn't a lack of pain. It's the strength to
endure it without becoming angry and bitter. I wish
I could understand you. Your mother says you were
a believer once. What happened to you?''

"Did my mother tell you about my God-fearing,
lying, cheating father?''

The hatred and bitterness in his tone shocked
Amanda to her soul. He always sounded angry whenever the subject of God or prayer came up but now
he sounded as if he were a different man. Amanda
could do no more than shake her head.

"I didn't think so. If I had any faith, he killed it.''
Garth's eyes seemed to blaze brighter with every
word he spoke. "The way he almost killed my
mother.''

"I don't understand.''

"Did she tell you about him?''

"Only that he was demanding and that he asked
too much of you and your sister sometimes.''

"Sometimes? Try twenty-four hours a day. None
of us ever measured up or were perfect enough for
him. He was a very godly man,'' Garth said sarcas-
tically. "An elder in the church. He—'' Garth broke
off and started to turn away but Amanda reached out
to stop him.

"I'd like to understand,'' she said.

"He took a lover. One of the women who worked
in the church office. He was the church treasurer and
she worked with him. When Mom found out and
confronted him, he didn't deny it or say he was sorry.
He told her he'd been waiting until I graduated from

high school to tell her. He had it all figured out. She was supposed to leave him. Then in a couple years, he'd marry the woman who'd comforted him when Mom deserted him.''

Amanda's heart felt as if a fist were squeezing it. Something told her Garth's father's plans didn't go that way at all. ''What happened then?''

''He didn't know I'd heard. I went to the pastor. Told him what was going on under his nose. He asked Dad to give the woman up.''

''That's as it should have been, but what did that do to your relationship with him?''

''I never saw him again. He left the night the pastor called him in and confronted him. He never came back home. He moved in with *her*.''

''And your mother?''

''I take care of my mother. I did then and I do now. I've given her more than he ever did or could. I made a success of myself in spite of his opinion of me.''

Once again, Amanda noticed his emphasis on success measured only in terms of money and security. ''I meant that she doesn't seem to be bitter at all.''

''She *loved* him too much. She didn't realize it but she was under his thumb—brainwashed into believing everything he said. It was as if he had dominated her for so long that she couldn't think for herself. He tried to do the same thing to my sister and me. I think she might have gone along with him if I hadn't short-circuited his plans. She even visited him before he died. He asked forgiveness. Can you imagine that? Mom lost her home and most of her friends and came close to a breakdown because of him and he wanted her forgiveness. A day late and a dollar short, as far as I'm concerned.''

"He didn't ask to see you?"

"I didn't go! I wasn't listening to his lies. Nothing he could have said or done would have earned him my forgiveness.''

"Garth, it's never a day late or a dollar short to ask forgiveness. Surely you understand that. There's nothing any of us can do to earn forgiveness. It's a gift. To give and to receive. Look at the good thief. He asked forgiveness and Jesus promised him paradise. There wasn't anything the thief could do to earn it, hanging there on the cross the way he was, except ask. His repentance was enough.''

"So you're saying my father was forgiven all the wrongs he did. He destroyed all our lives and God just forgives him." Garth snapped his fingers. "Just like that!''

"Yes. Garth, you have to get over this idea that it was God who turned His back on you. It was your father. Not your Father in heaven but a man—a flawed man to be sure but we're all flawed. We're all sinners.''

Garth's gaze had lost none of its anger. "I guess you'd have gone. You'd have forgiven him."

Amanda shrugged. "I'd like to think I would but I don't know. He wasn't my father. It wasn't my mother he betrayed. I'm sure he disillusioned you on more levels than I can imagine. I can't judge what you did but I will tell you that you need to forgive him—for *you* not him. You need to undo the damage he's done to you so you can put it all behind you.

Hatred takes too much energy and is just too destructive to hang on to.''

Garth raised a sardonic eyebrow. "I'll never forgive that man, Amanda. Never. Besides, it *is* behind me. I'm a grown man who doesn't need childish crutches to get by. I do it on my own.''

"And it wears you down." Amanda smiled sadly and squeezed his hand where it lay on his thigh. She was tempted to bring up his aversion to love or at least talking about it but perhaps she'd pushed far enough already. "Just think about it, okay?"

Garth stared at their hands for a long minute then looked up into her eyes. Amanda had never seen his eyes look so stormy but it wasn't anger that churned in their blue depths. She had no idea what it was— but anger it wasn't. And it made her nervous.

"Didn't you say something about going home?" She stood before he could voice the emotion she saw in his turbulent blue gaze.

Garth blinked. "I hoped maybe we could stop for dinner. I didn't get time to grab lunch and breakfast was forgettable.''

"Sounds good," Amanda said. It meant the possibility of good food, which with Frieda around was in short supply, and more time in Garth's company. That was a combination that she just couldn't bear to turn down no matter how tired she was. "I didn't have dinner, either, and lunch was...*very* forgettable.''

Garth groaned on her behalf. "Don't tell me my mother brought lunch in again when she visited Jason today.''

"I didn't have the heart to turn her down and I

thought this time it would be okay.'' Amanda wrinkled her nose. ''I just don't understand how anyone could ruin egg salad.''

''It's the cloves. She insists they add something. I think she was born without taste or smell or something.'' Garth chuckled. ''Sweetheart, you're going to have to risk hurting her feelings. It isn't going to get any better. You're the only person I've ever known who's eaten what she cooks for this long and lived to tell the sad story.''

''I...I...ahem...'' Shocked by the endearment, Amanda paused to recover. ''I'd hate to make her feel bad.''

''She ought to be used to it by now.'' Garth smiled in the darkness that engulfed them as they entered the parking garage. *Sweetheart* had just slipped out but it had really rattled her. He'd found he enjoyed rattling the unshakable Amanda. Then a troublesome thought struck. *Why did I call her sweetheart?*

Chapter Seven

"No! No, wait!" Jason sat up straighter in bed. "Don't turn it off yet. Look! Isn't that where Dad flew those guys?" he asked.

Amanda looked up and watched with cold dread as the weatherman explained that sudden fierce thunderstorms had developed over western Pennsylvania and West Virginia. She remembered how anxious Garth had been about the day's itinerary. This was the first flight Liberty Express would make ferrying the executive of a large agriculture products company based outside Philadelphia. It was the company Garth had been meeting with the day Jason had found out the truth about who she was. It was hard for Amanda not to resent the CEO of the company for leaving orders not to be disturbed. It was because of him that it had taken Garth two hours to reach the hospital.

"What's wind shear, Mom?" Jason asked, dragging Amanda back to the present.

"Wind shear? Oh, I missed that. What did they say?"

"That the airports were still open but that pilots had reported wind shear and they have light craft warnings in effect."

"I think it's some sort of weird wind that makes flying difficult," Amanda answered as nonchalantly as possible. All the while her mind flooded with memories of large airliners whose crashes had been blamed on wind shear. "I don't know much about that sort of thing." Her stomach muscles felt like quick-setting concrete. What if Garth tried to fly in that? Wasn't his plane considered a light craft? And he was already an hour late.

"Hey, Mom, don't worry. Dad knows what he's doing."

Amanda stared at Jason, trying to decide if she'd frightened him. "I—I'm not the least bit worried."

Jason nodded gravely. "Sure," he said sounding unconvinced. He pushed away his barely touched dinner tray. "I can't eat this stuff. Did they hire Grandmom as a cook?"

Amanda forced a chuckle, though his continued lack of appetite wasn't good. "That's not nice."

"Neither is Grandmom's cooking," Jason quipped with an exaggerated grimace. "Let's finish the game we started."

Two hours later, Jason looked up from his board game. "I'm worried now, too, Mom. Dad always calls when he's going to be late. Maybe you could call his office. They might have heard something."

"What a good idea! Now, why didn't I think of

that?'' Amanda pounced on the phone and punched out the number.

It rang twice. "Liberty Express, Marge speaking." Garth's secretary sounded as anxious as Amanda was.

"It's Amanda, Marge. Jason and I wondered if you've heard from Garth."

"Not since they landed in New Castle. That was around noon. They still had quite a jaunt ahead of them. The boss'll be beat when he gets in. I'll have him call as soon as he lands. Are you planning to stay with Jason until then?''

"Yes. Yes, I am. I'm sorry if I bothered you. Jason was worried. Is anything wrong?''

"Now don't get upset but Garth's plane is…is…"

"Is? Is what?''

"The tower at Pittsburgh lost contact with Garth. But he'd said he was going to try to put down somewhere outside the storm's path. It was pretty fierce out there and communication was patchy." Marge took a deep breath. "Please don't worry. He's a wonderful pilot. Remind Jason that Garth's an ace. That man was practically born with wings. He's probably sitting out the worst of it in some drafty hangar. He wouldn't want you two to worry."

Amanda hung up knowing she couldn't tell Jason the full truth even though Marge had been wrong. Amanda wasn't just worried. She was frantic. She remembered with stunning clarity Garth's final words to her in the chapel after the wedding. *Pilots aren't that different from cops…some of us never come home from work again, either. Who knows, maybe*

I'll go down in flames one of these days, and you'll be rid of me.

She'd never bothered to deny that she might want to be rid of him.

"Miss Marge hasn't heard from him either, huh?"

"Not in a while," Amanda said casually, "but last she heard he planned to wait out the storms on the ground."

Jason shook his head. "Uh-uh. Dad told me last night that he had to get the men where they were going or he'd have to pay the plumber." Jason stopped, screwing up his face. "No, that wasn't it."

Amanda felt her heart sink as Jason's meaning became clear. "You mean the piper? He'd have to pay the piper?" she asked.

Jason nodded then added quickly, "But like I said, Dad's the best pilot in the world. If anyone could get them there safe, it's Dad."

Amanda smiled. She knew Jason was worried and trying to protect her. She'd seen him do it countless times with Garth and, like Garth, she hid the fear lurking in her heart as best she could. *What if no one could have flown through those storms safely?*

Garth jogged across the street from the parking garage. He grimaced when the sun burned through the fog with a sudden burst of light and heat. Marge said Amanda had sounded worried because no one had heard from him. And that had been last night.

Amanda must be frantic by now. Garth smiled as it occurred to him for one selfish second that if Amanda was worried, it might mean she cared for him as more than just the man who'd raised her son.

But he banished the joy. He hated the thought that Amanda had suffered a second's distress on his account. He had no right to be glad if she'd begun to care because there was no future for them.

The remark he'd made after the wedding about the dangers of his job had echoed in his mind all night as he cooled his heels at Mayport Field. The tiny airfield in the mountains of West Virginia was just a fly speck on the map and consisted of an army surplus Quonset hut and three sheds. The storms had been right on his tail and Henry Mayport lost telephone communication and power before Garth could tie down his plane. Phone service had still been out that morning when he'd taken off.

He'd paced all night thinking about that snide remark. He should have explained that his profession was less dangerous than many. There were even statistics he could have cited that said more men were killed in cars going to nice, safe office jobs than were killed working as pilots.

Garth found Amanda in the solarium near Jason's room. She was curled up in a big chair, hugging her legs, her head on her up-drawn knees, her thick hair hiding her face. Garth knelt next to her and pushed back her tousled hair. Her eyes were shadowed after what the nurse on duty said had been a sleepless night. Garth smiled gently. "Amanda... Mandy," he whispered. "Wake up, sweetheart."

Amanda's head shot up. "Garth! You're okay! Oh, thank you, Lord."

Garth couldn't believe his good fortune when Amanda launched herself against his chest and hugged him for all she was worth. But before he'd even had time to enjoy the feel of her in his arms, she pulled away, jumped up and glared at him. "Why didn't you call? Do you have any idea how worried I...J-Jason was."

He stood and leaned against the back of the chair. He just couldn't suppress a grin he felt grow on his face. He'd heard the admission she'd unsuccessfully covered. And she wasn't getting away with it. He raised an eyebrow and crossed his arms. "Jason was? Or you were? Which is it?" he taunted playfully.

"Both! How could you do it? How could you put your life in danger for business? For money? You could have been killed! And for what? A company. Success! If your crash had been worse, you'd all be dead!"

Garth frowned. "Crash? What crash?"

"Now what crash do you think I'm talking about?"

Garth spread his hands helplessly. "I don't know what you're talking about."

"Play dumb, then!" Amanda shouted and planted her hands on her hips. "But I know you crash-landed before you could get to the Pittsburgh airport. They told Marge and Marge told me."

"No!"

Tears filled Amanda's eyes and she furiously scrubbed them away. "Don't lie!"

"I do not lie!"

"They told her they lost contact with you, so you may as well tell me the truth."

"Amanda, listen to me," Garth demanded, losing his patience a bit more each time she accused him of lying. "They lost contact with me because I turned back and flew out of their range. I was trying to get away from the storms. Another storm pattern cropped up in my path so I headed into West Virginia instead of back to Ohio. I set down at a little field in the mountains."

Amanda was clearly confused. "But...but you told Jason you had to get those men where they were going. You *had* to keep flying!"

Garth was shocked to utter silence by the certainty in her tone. There was more going on here than worry, his careless remarks or her reaction to them.

"You wouldn't give up!" she continued. "It wouldn't matter to you one bit that Jason was here worrying." Amanda paused for a breath to continue her diatribe. "*Jason* who isn't supposed to get upset. *Jason* who is the only reason you got into this stupid marriage."

Garth felt sudden defeat weigh him down. Why had he ever let hope glimmer into his heart that perhaps he could make her happy? That, perhaps, he could make their marriage work. He'd made her miserable from the day he'd met her. Since before he'd met her considering that he'd had Jason while she'd longed for her son. Why did she have to make him care!

Cold anger replaced hurt and defeat and Garth was thankful for his irrational feelings. "You could have explained my absence last night by saying I'd stayed over in another city. You could have saved Jason all the worry you say he suffered. Now if you'll excuse me, I'd like to go reassure him. And I'd appreciate time alone with him. I missed my visit last night."

Amanda watched Garth stalk out of the solarium,

then sat down in defeat. She hadn't meant to anger him but perhaps that was better than his figuring out why she hadn't been able to lie to Jason. Why she hadn't been able to hide her own worry or think clearly enough to formulate a simple lie.

She loved him.

And she'd thought she'd lost him.

And now that Amanda had faced that truth, she had to face another. He hadn't even tried to call. He hadn't even thought of her. There really was every possibility that, to him, she was just a means to keep Jason. One thing was a certainty. She had fallen in love with a man just like her late husband. Jess wouldn't have called, either.

After two hours, Amanda wandered down the hall to Jason's room. Tired and emotionally spent, she arrived just as Dr. Matt Hernandez did. He put his arm around her shoulders, misinterpreting her despondency. "Hey. Cheer up. I know Jason looks bad but it's not any worse than usual. And I come bearing good news for a change. Jason's ready. We can do the transplant tomorrow. See Cindy before she goes home and she'll give you your instructions."

"Do I stay in the hospital tonight?"

Hernandez shook his head. "That's not necessary. Have Garth bring you in by six. You'll be prepped and ready by seven." The oncologist put his hand on her shoulder. "Come on! Cheer up! This is it! It's all downhill from here."

Amanda forced a smile. "Right. Downhill. Let's tell Jason." She pushed open the door.

"Come on. Open that tunnel wide," Garth told Jason as he tried to coax him to eat with an absurd-looking spoon. The handle was shaped like a train with a spoon on the end. The electronic sound of a train echoed through the room. Absurd though it was, Jason giggled, opened his mouth and ate some Jell-O.

"You don't eat for me like that," she accused mildly.

Jason gave her a wan smile. "I'm a train tunnel. At lunch I get to be an airplane hangar."

Matt picked up the box containing the airplane spoon, dumped it out and activated the engine noise. "These are great, Garth," he said. "Especially now. Jason needs to build up his strength if he's going to be hitting home runs again soon. And since tomorrow is his transplant, I'd say the other teams better get ready for some competition."

"Tomorrow?" Garth asked.

"Tomorrow?" Jason asked at the same time.

"Tomorrow. Garth, you need to have Amanda here by six. The lab's been scheduled and I've got the best man to work on Amanda. It's easy stuff for Jason here. Just like another transfusion for you, fella."

"And then I'll be better?" Jason asked, his eyes suddenly bright.

"Then we test every day and watch that cell count start climbing." He unrolled a plastic sheet that had the outline of what looked like a three-foot high thermometer printed on it. "We'll hang this chart on the wall for you to color in. You'll be able to chart your own progress. You can fill in every healthy new blood cell you grow. Right now your thermometer's nearly empty. First few days, the rest go. Then afte a while they'll start building again. When it's all full, we'll start talking about when you get to go home!''

"Home." Jason sighed. He sounded like poor Dorothy pining for Kansas.

Amanda glanced at Garth for the first time. He hadn't said a word and sat looking pensive. The anger had disappeared from his expressive eyes. "How long do you think it will be before we see some results?" he asked, speaking at last.

Hernandez glanced at all three of them. "Okay, this is how we count. Today's day minus one. Tomorrow's day zero. The next is day plus one. At day plus fourteen we should see a small change in the cell count. That cell count will get higher every day. Right, pal?'' He tugged on the brim of Jason's red Phillies cap.

"Right!''

Garth heard it again. There was a loose board under the wall-to-wall carpet in Amanda's room that squeaked whenever someone stepped on it. Considering the rhythm of the squeaks he'd guess she was pacing.

Guilt assailed him. They hadn't had a chance to talk alone. Not about their disagreement or even tomorrow's procedure. His sister had come in then his mother arrived just as Christina was leaving. He'd had to get back to Liberty Express for a meeting with his accountant and his mother had promised to take Amanda home.

k. Sque-e-e-ak!

oise set Garth's teeth on edge. This had to it looked like it might be up to him to put a stop to Amanda's pacing. He'd realized, as he watched Amanda's mixed reaction to the transplant being scheduled, that he'd been foolish to react to her anger with a show of his own. There had to be a reason for her to fly off the handle, and instead of probing gently, he'd acted like the proverbial bull in a china shop. He hadn't even explained that he'd tried to call.

Squeak. Sque-e-e-ak!

Garth threw back the covers and pulled on a pair of jeans. Neither one of them was going to get any sleep tonight if they didn't talk. He tapped on the connecting door. "Amanda?"

Squeak.

Silence. Garth smiled. "Come on, Amanda, I know you're awake. I've heard you pacing."

Sque-e-e-ak! "Oops," Amanda muttered.

Garth chuckled. "I'm coming in so I hope you're decent. If you're not, better cover up." He pushed open the door in time to see her toss a robe over a long T-shirt and sit on the side of the bed. She looked up and Garth was horrified to see how pale she was. "Good heavens, Amanda, are you ill?"

"No."

She wouldn't even look at him. "You aren't still upset about this morning, are you? Look, I'm sorry I snapped back at you. I should have remembered that you'd had a bad night. I should have told you that I couldn't call because the storm knocked out communications before I got to the hangar." Amanda remained silent.

Garth sighed. He hated seeing her like this. "Amanda," he said as he walked to the bed then sat next to her. Being closer didn't help. Garth could feel the tension coming off her in waves but he could only see the top of her head. "What is it? And don't say nothing."

He tried to think and nothing came to mind. She'd hugged him for all she was worth that morning then her mood had done a one-eighty and she'd nearly taken his head off. He put his crooked knuckle under her chin and encouraged her to look at him. Her violet eyes were almost glazed. "Amanda, you're acting—"

"Crazy?" she asked.

Incredulous, Garth stared at her for a full five seconds. "Amanda, you are not crazy!"

Fire flared in the violet depths of her eyes. "What do you think of someone who'd rather go through twenty hours of labor without anything for pain rather than have anyone come near her with a needle? Don't placate me! Go ahead. Tell me that's not crazy."

"That's not crazy! *Karen* was unbalanced. *You* have a phobia."

"Phobia, schmobia! This is my son's life and I'm sitting in here shaking in my slippers, wishing tomorrow just wouldn't come. I feel so stupid and so incredibly selfish."

A fat tear rolled from one of her eyes and tracked across her cheek. Garth couldn't help himself. He leaned forward and captured it with a soft kiss. He sat back quickly. That felt too close, too real, for their temporary marriage.

"You are *not* selfish," he told her. "Not once have you flinched from doing what was best for Jason. Well, you weren't too crazy about marrying me, but it's not your fault you resented me because I'd been raising Jason.''

Amanda shook her head. ''Oh, don't think that. I don't resent you. You've been a wonderful father to him. Anyone can see that.''

''Well, I'm sure not your ideal husband.''

''But that's not because you're not attractive or nice.''

Garth barely resisted the urge to groan. Nice! Why did she always have to think of him as nice. There was nothing wrong with nice, of course. His mother had raised him to be—well—nice. He held out his arms and she came to him, leaning and snuggling against him. Garth smiled against her hair and stroked her back. She sighed and relaxed. No, there was nothing wrong with nice at all.

They sat that way with Garth murmuring comforting words and caressing her back and hair until Amanda raised her face to his. ''I'll be fine alone. You must be tired, Garth.''

''No more tired than you. I managed to catch a few hours of shut-eye. From what I've heard, you were up pacing all last night, too. Come on, get under the covers and scoot over to make room for me.''

''But—''

''Amanda, I'm not going to get a wink of sleep unless I'm sure you're okay and sleeping soundly. I'm not here to make demands. I came in here to find out what was wrong and how to help. Now move over a bit.'' Garth settled next to her, heavy jeans and all.

She sat staring at him, wide-eyed and shocked. "But—" she said again.

Garth slid down in bed then reached up and put one fingertip to her lips. "Sh-sh. Just trust me." He wove his arm behind her, cupped her head with the palm of his hand and pulled her down so that her head rested on his shoulder. With his other arm he stretched to turn off the light, plunging the room into darkness.

"Did I ever tell you about the Saturday Jason woke up early when he was almost six?" Garth asked in a hushed tone. "They'd learned about not littering in kindergarten the day before. He apparently looked out and saw the Saturday paper on our lawn. He snuck out so he wouldn't wake us and *cleaned* up the lawn. Once he picked up our newspaper, he wondered if everyone else had papers littering their lawns, too.

"Mom and I woke up about an hour later to find twenty newspapers in trash bags in the kitchen. It took another hour to get the paperboy on the phone, get the house numbers he'd delivered, then to go and ask everyone if their papers were missing."

Amanda smiled in the darkness. "Were they angry?"

"No, not really. They thought it was funny. So did we."

Garth chuckled. "Then there was what Mother calls the popcorn incident. He was about four and a half. We were lucky he wasn't hurt. You see, he'd read a book about popcorn. He was reading by then which was pretty scary since we didn't teach him. Well, anyway, in the book, the bear parents went out and left the children alone and they decided to make popcorn.''

''What did he do?''

''Fortunately, Jason didn't fill the house with popcorn even though he used enough to. Unfortunately, my mother has nothing on him when it comes to kitchen disasters. The book didn't give a recipe. He put about four inches of oil into the bottom of an old pressure cooker we use to pop popcorn. Then he dumped the whole bag of popping corn in and turned the mess on.

''I'd been flying all night and had probably been asleep three hours when he climbed up on the bed and woke me. Jason never likes to upset people so he starts explaining things gently. 'I opened all the windows and doors but I can't get the smoke out of the house.' I catapulted out of bed like I'd been shot from a cannon.''

Amanda chuckled so Garth launched into another and yet another story. He spoke in soft, quiet tones as he ran his fingers softly through her hair. He talked about funny incidents, heartwarming moments and his hopes and dreams for Jason's future. After nearly an hour, Amanda's breathing changed, slowed, deepened. She slept at last and, exhausted, Garth let his own eyes drift closed. He gave himself up to the joy of feeling Amanda in his arms as soft tendrils of sleep wrapped around him in the darkness. He didn't even realize where his last thoughts went.

Could you find a way for it to always be like this, Lord? Please.

Chapter Eight

~🍂~

Amanda climbed her way out of the mists of sleep toward the far-off sound of a buzzer. At first she thought it was a fire alarm but the smell that greeted her wasn't smoke. It was sandalwood and spice. Garth's unique aftershave.

She forced her grainy eyes open and noticed the dent in the pillow next to her. Heat rushed to her cheeks as she hit the snooze bar on her alarm clock. She didn't want to get up. She wanted to pull the covers over her head rather than face Garth. She'd acted like such a fool last night! Crying and shaking over today's procedure.

Amanda shook her head ruefully. Some witness to the peace of the Lord she was. It was a good thing He didn't rely on mortal men to fill His kingdom. If He did, at the end of time it would be a pretty empty place.

But then Amanda remembered that it was by the deed and actions of men that Garth had judged God.

What kind of confidence had she shown in His power?

Amanda bowed her head. *Lord, please watch over me this day. Pour out Your peace on me and show Garth how mighty a God You are by healing our son. And, Lord, if You could work on his heart about the sanctity of marriage I'd appreciate it. I love him and I don't want to lose him even though he confuses me. He's such a good person. This plan he has to just walk away from me and his vows doesn't fit. I know he's Yours, Lord. Please show him the way back to You.*

A noise drew Amanda's attention. She looked up as Garth peaked his head in the door. He smiled. "Feeling better this morning?"

Panic once again flooded Amanda, washing away all thought but one. The transplant! Needles! Long needles! Great big, fat needles! Amanda shuddered.

"Calm down," Garth said, his smile gone, compassion in his gaze. "You're going to be fine."

Amanda tightened her grip on the blankets and with it her control over her runaway emotions. "What I'm probably going to do is make an idiot of myself again. What I'm *not* going to do is let it stop me," she promised.

Garth walked to the bed and sat next to her, his hand resting on her knee. "I never thought for one moment that wild horses could stop you from doing anything you could to help your son—or anyone else for that matter."

Amanda smiled, warmed by his regard. "Thank you," she said and continued trying to sound confident. "And don't worry about me. I'll be just fine today."

Evidently Garth saw right through her bravado. "If you need me I'll stay with you. Just let me know."

"Jason's going to need you more than I do, Garth. He's not as confident as he pretends." Amanda lay her hand over his. "I'll get through this with the Lord's help. I always have in the past."

"You shouldn't have to rely on some distant entity that you can't see."

"But I can feel His presence and His peace when I don't let my own fear overwhelm me."

"Like last night?"

"No. Last night I forgot to stop and listen to His voice inside me. I'm afraid I've been doing that a lot lately. But He took care of me anyway. He sent you to me. You helped me get through the night."

"You frustrate me. Do you know that?"

"How?"

"Because I want to believe you when you say things like that." Amanda felt his hand ball into a tight, quaking fist under her palm. "But I just can't."

Amanda smiled and gently squeezed that hard, frustrated fist under her hand. "You're a hard nut to crack. I'll give you that. But you'll crack. He has His hand on your life, Garth. Mine too. He's intertwined them for some purpose. We just don't know what it is yet."

Garth rubbed his free hand over his face. "Enough of the metaphysical at 5:00 a.m., okay?"

She moved her hand to his arm, giving him another gentle squeeze. "I can't explain it, but I know something good will come of all this."

"I'm sorry, Amanda, but I can't imagine anything good coming out of this mess. But I do have an idea that I believe would help get you through today." His eyes suddenly went serious and his smile faded. "Every time you feel yourself start to panic during the procedure, think about Jason. Not the Jason you've come to know." He pulled a picture out of his pocket and handed it to her. "This is Jason. It was taken just before he got sick."

In the picture her son had a full head of gleaming hair and a bright, sunny smile. He was hanging upside down from a rung on the ladder to his now deserted tree house.

"The kid's part monkey. Maybe we'll find out he's part cat, too. That would give him at least one life left, right?"

Amanda nodded and just stared at the picture. Something good had to come of all the suffering this boy had faced in the past year. It had to!

"Are you sure she's all right?" Garth asked the pretty young nurse at the desk. He'd known Maria Hernandez for five years. She'd worked her way through nursing school as his part-time secretary. It was through her that he'd found Jason's oncologist. Matt was her brother.

Maria hissed something under her breath, then looked up from the chart. "What did I tell you five minutes ago?"

"That she was fine," Garth admitted.

She nodded. "That's what I said, but I also promised to tell you if anything changed. She was fine then and she still is. Have you got any reason to believe I'd lie to you?''

Garth shrugged. ''You might not want to upset me.''

Maria Hernandez sighed. ''You ought to know me better than that. I don't give a hang if you're upset. Now leave me alone with my charts. You know I hate paperwork, Garth Jorgensen.''

Garth knew. He also knew he was acting like a complete fool but he couldn't seem to help himself. All he could see in his mind's eye was Amanda's pale face, her eyes full of fear and the brave smile she'd plastered on her face as he'd left her. ''She's afraid. Is this going to hurt?''

''Ah! A way to prove that I'll tell you the truth. Sorry to say it's going to hurt plenty.''

''Nurse Hernandez,'' Jason's oncologist growled from behind Garth. ''We do not frighten already worried family members.''

''We do when they act loco, *mi hermano!*''

Matt Hernandez chuckled and turned from his sister to Garth. ''I was down there a little while ago. Amanda said to tell you she's fine. That sometimes facing a fear is the only way to get over it.''

Garth sighed and raked his fingers through his hair. ''But is she fine or trying to ease my mind? She's like that.''

''*She's fine.* I thought you were going to stay with Jason.''

''He's with my mother. He wanted me to find out about Amanda.''

Hernandez laughed. "I just left Jason. He tossed you out! Come on. Let's get you something to eat."

Garth felt his face heat. "No, I'll go back and tell Jason Amanda's doing okay." Riding the elevator back up the three floors to Jason's isolation room, he couldn't help wishing that he'd asked to be allowed to stay with Amanda.

"Hey, kiddo," Garth said when he pushed the door open to find his mother and Jason collaborating on a game of solitaire. Jason was so weak it broke his heart. "We're almost there," he told his son. "Your mom's getting through this like a real trouper. They'll be up within the hour. Doctor Matt was in, I hear?"

"He said the same thing about Mom." Jason eyed Garth with suspicion. "Are you going to play now or keep hopping up and down?"

Garth chuckled then rubbed his hands together. "I was only trying to distract you. But since you've thwarted my scheme, I'll just have to beat you fair and square."

Jason grinned. "In your dreams. I'm Monopoly champ of the hospital."

"You hear this smart-mouthed kid, Mom? I think it's time to take him down a peg or two."

"Oh, at least two," Frieda Jorgensen agreed. "I think I'll go get a cup of coffee and a cruller."

Garth didn't protest. He knew wearing a surgical mask and gown bothered his elderly mother but while Jason had no ability to fight infection they had to be extra careful. Jason was too listless to play more than one trip around the board so Garth got out the crossword puzzle book and pretended to be in dire need of his help. Jason fell asleep in the middle of the first puzzle.

He never even woke when the transfusion bag of precious bone marrow arrived. He slept while the transfusion was hooked into a line that had been fed through a vein in his arm to a place near his heart. It was through that line that he was fed, infused with medication, transfused and now given the marrow Amanda donated. It couldn't start working fast enough for Garth.

Amanda arrived half an hour later looking wan yet cheerful. Still, Garth couldn't help but worry about her. She stood by Jason's side but soon retreated to a chair. As the minutes rolled by she put her head back and drifted off to sleep. It was only then that her face began to mirror increasing levels of pain. Garth finally couldn't take it anymore and gave in to the uncontrollable urge to cosset her. He walked over and crouched down in front of her.

"Amanda," he whispered and took her hand in his. "Come on. Let's get you home."

Her eyes popped open quickly but were glazed with pain. "No, I haven't even talked to him yet today. I should be here. I'm fine. Really."

In a pig's eye, Garth thought, remembering Matt's warning that she would be in considerable pain. "Then let's go grab lunch. Jason hasn't moved a muscle. He'll sleep that long for sure."

Amanda looked like a deer caught in a bright pair of headlights. He stood and offered her his hand. She tried gamely to stand but sank back down, shaking from the pain. Garth shook his head and squatted down to his previous position.

"How come you're so stubborn? You hurt, Mandy. Didn't your doctor tell you he'd give you something for pain?"

"I don't like pain medication. Besides, he's next door by now. I'll be fine. It just took me by surprise."

"Next door? You mean at the adult hospital?"

She nodded and Garth stood. "I'll be right back."

Amanda watched Garth stalk out. Was he angry or concerned? She never knew what he was thinking where she was concerned, yet she could practically read his mind when his thoughts were on Jason. It was darn frustrating. She got her answer minutes later when he returned with a wheelchair. The look in his eyes was gentle, his brow creased with worry.

"Come on, Mandy. It's past time someone looked after you. Chris is on her way in. She'll stay with Jason."

"You—you're going to look after me?"

He carefully scooped her up. "You have a problem with that?" he asked and smirked as if to say *Do you have a choice?*

Amanda sighed and dropped her head on his shoulder. "No. No problem at all."

Garth lowered her into the chair and she felt suddenly bereft without the shelter of his arms surrounding her. She'd been alone so long. A tear trickled down her cheek. Amanda quickly wiped it away but another replaced it on the other cheek. Garth smoothed that one away. "Poor Mandy. You've had a heck of a time lately." He kissed the top of her head and started the wheelchair forward. "But I'm here now to take care of you."

Amanda closed her eyes and prayed he always would be.

Hours later Garth paced across the room then returned and stood next to Amanda's bed to watch her pale face once again as she slept. She lay so frighteningly still. He smoothed a stray lock of hair off her forehead, then traced her delicate features with his eyes then his fingertips.

"I love you," he whispered. "I didn't want to. I can't tell you that I do but that doesn't mean I don't. It just means that I'm no good for you. Funny, isn't it? I've crash-landed a 727 in a swamp and I wasn't anywhere near as terrified as I am of ruining your life more than I already have. I just can't take the thought of failing you the way my father failed me."

"Garth," he heard his sister call softly from the doorway. "Is Amanda all right?"

"She's sleeping," Garth answered not taking his eyes off his wife.

"Then what's wrong? You look troubled."

Not willing to reveal his inner torment he voiced a lesser worry. "It's just that she's sleeping so soundly. They gave her a shot and it must have helped because she fell asleep."

Chris shrugged. "So, she's asleep. The shot will probably take time to wear off."

"That's what the nurse said but it's been hours."

"Come across the hall and I'll tell you about Jason."

Garth nodded but didn't move. "Why wouldn't she tell me she was in pain? Why did I have to guess?"

"Come on. I think we need to talk." Chris took his arm and marched him across the hall to the solarium. The news about Jason was that he was still sleeping peacefully but Chris had Garth's welfare on her mind. "Why do you think Amanda didn't tell you how bad she felt?"

"I don't have a clue," Garth answered, confused.

Chris blew her bangs off her forehead with a furious puff of air. "You're right. You don't have a clue. About anything! She probably didn't tell you because she assumed you were more interested in Jason."

"I'm interested in her, too," Garth grumbled.

"Sit," Chris ordered and took his hand after settling across from him. "Don't you think it's time you told her just how much you care?"

"No. I can't do that. I promised her this arrangement was temporary. It's the only way. I want her to be happy."

"Amanda's been alone a lot of years. Do you really think she wants to stay that way?"

Garth grimaced. "Well, as much as I'd like to be the one to change all that, I'm not the man for the job." Garth slumped down in the sofa. "I'm just not good at making women happy."

"What?" Chris asked, incredulous.

"I failed Karen miserably, Chris. You know that! I swore I'd never be like our father and then when the going got tough I asked her for a separation. And because of that, she stole Jason from Amanda. I was so wrapped up in my own needs that I didn't notice that she was sick. I'm afraid that stealing Jason was her way of trying to hold on to me."

"Are all men this stupid or does it just run in our family?" Chris let go of his hand and slapped the arm of her chair. "Karen was a deeply troubled person! She had no conscience, no sense of right and wrong. She was like a spoiled child until the day she died. She stole that boy to get you back. Because she had to have every toy she wanted. She might only want to break it but no one else could have it. That's all you were to her. A toy. A pet. Then she realized she couldn't have you and she decided to break you instead. When she couldn't do that, she decided to destroy Jason to get at you but Mom stopped her from taking him with her that day."

She reached out and gripped Garth's hand, frowning at him, willing him to hear her. "You didn't fail at your marriage. You tried everything in your power to help her—but she didn't want help. She didn't want to change. Don't let her succeed in ruining the rest of your life. This is your chance for true happiness. You can't let it slip through your fingers. You love Amanda."

Chris held up her hand like a traffic cop to stop his denial. "Don't. I saw your face in the mirror when I came in to her room. I'm great at lipreading."

Restless and uncomfortable, Garth stood and wandered to the window and sat on the wide sill. "But Amanda's probably counting the days until she can divorce me and have Jason mostly to herself."

"Amanda's a true Christian, brother mine, so I'm sure she doesn't take her marriage vows that lightly."

"But divorcing eventually was part of our arrangement. As for her calling herself a Christian, is that supposed to mean something to me? Our father was always talking about serving God and it didn't stop him from divorcing our mother. Besides which, her religion is more of a deterrent than a recommendation. And it goes both ways before you say I'm prejudiced.''

Chris pinched the bridge of her nose and sighed. "It isn't a religion. It's belief in Jesus Christ."

"It's hogwash," Garth muttered.

"I'm not going to get into this debate with you again. It's a waste of breath." Chris's blue eyes flashed as she stood. "Sometimes I can't believe Mom raised such an idiot," she added in a far more loving tone. She touched his shoulder and strode out of the room.

Amanda rolled over and a dull ache in her pelvis brought her awake. In the dimly lit room, she could just make out the dial of her watch. "Dinnertime," she mumbled and sat up. A shadow at the corner of her vision made her gasp.

Garth sat forward and smiled. Amanda felt her traitorous heart skip. "Welcome back to the land of the living."

Amanda's head felt muzzy, her eyes dry, her mouth like cotton. "What happened?"

"They gave you something for pain that should have put you out for three, maybe four hours. You've been asleep for twelve. It's 6:00 a.m."

"It's morning? Then why are you here?"

He raised an eyebrow. "I wanted to be."

"Oh."

* * *

Two hours later, Amanda sat curled up with a blanket on the wide windowsill of the solarium down the hall from Jason's isolation room. Normally, during the afternoon hours it was full of children. The sounds of their delicate laughter echoed in her mind and tortured her. Jason hadn't laughed today. He just lay still, his eyes listless and dull. He was so sick. She hadn't been prepared for just how sick he would be.

She hadn't understood.

Wiping the tears that tracked down her cheeks, she turned toward the sound of footsteps in the hall. Garth, his face creased with worry, stood just outside the door. "He—" His voice cracked and he tried again. "He fell asleep."

Amanda's lip quivered and another tear fell. "I beat him at Monopoly. Oh, Garth. What if it doesn't work? I never asked. What happens then?"

Garth walked toward her and she went to him. "It has to work. This can't all be in vain. It can't." He gathered her in his arms. "Are you feeling any better today?"

Amanda nodded, her head bobbing against Garth's chest. He's right, she thought. This has to work. It just has to! *Oh please, Father, make Jason get better. Give him back to us.* Amanda glanced up at Garth's strained face. *And please, let Garth see Your power and compassion through Jason. Use all this pain for good.*

Garth stared out into the night remembering the last two weeks. He'd felt as if he'd been living in a nightmare. So had Amanda. So had Jason. Jason's discomfort, due to the side effects of the transplant, had been extreme. Garth had sat with Jason in his lap one night for hours before sleep finally slipped under the pain. Since that day, the only nourishment he'd been able to get was through IV feedings. His weight had gone down to forty pounds. Transfusions of packed red cells and hemoglobin had been practically all that kept him alive.

But today he'd taken an uphill turn. It was a small step on the long road to recovery, but Garth would never forget the moment when he'd fully understood what Matt was saying....

Matt Hernandez sat in a chair at the base of Jason's bed, studying that day's test results. Garth and Amanda stood next to Jason on either side of the bed. It was a moment fraught with tension and hope. Hernandez looked up. A wide smile graced his features. "We've got a white cell count!"

Garth looked up from Jason's puzzled face into Amanda's eyes. They were once again flooded with tears. But this time they were tears of joy.

"Is that good? Does that mean I can go home soon?" Jason asked.

"Slow down there, pal. This is just the start. You've got to give it time," the doctor explained.

"How much time?"

Garth laughed. "What's this, kiddo? A new version of, 'Are we almost there?' You know we told you that you could be here for three more months."

"The rest of your time here will go by so fast you won't believe it," Amanda promised. "Every day you'll feel better, stronger. We'll play games with you and I'll bring you books and arts and crafts projects to do.''

"But I want to come home and be a family.''

Garth sat down next to the bed. "We're a family right here. A house doesn't make it happen.''

The scene blurred in Garth's mind and his eyes focused on the present. He saw Amanda's reflection in the window behind him where she sat on the sofa in the home Jason longed for. She was doing something with her hands, her graceful fingers moving over the material she held. "What's that?'' he asked.

"Jason asked for his own pajamas. Everything he has is way too big in the waist. So I'm putting drawstrings in the waistband with the elastic. That way he can grow into them again without realizing how much weight he's lost.''

"Maybe we could get him a pair of sweats with a drawstring to wear when he comes home.''

"It sounds like such a long way away,'' Amanda lamented.

Garth chuckled. "You're as bad as Jason.''

"I've always been impatient for things to happen. I guess he gets it from me.''

Garth walked over and sat on the end of the sofa. "What was his father like? What does Jason get from him?''

Amanda frowned, deep in thought. "I don't know. I've never seen Jason healthy except as an infant and I don't think I ever saw Jess sick. Or sit *still* for that matter. He was always on the go. He was a bit of an oddity in a town on the edge of the bayou. Hardly anybody over the age of twelve moved if they didn't have to.''

"That's how I noticed Jason was sick. He was never still, either, until then.''

Amanda smiled wistfully. "I don't think he slept six hours a day when he was an infant. I bet no mother in New Orleans was more exhausted than I was.''

"How did you and your husband wind up in New Orleans?''

"Dreams. Young love. I wanted to go to a school in the city and Jess wanted to be a big-city police officer. When my parents died, Jess offered to put me through college. He'd already been accepted to the New Orleans Police Academy. We got married and moved to the city. After I graduated, I worked for a while then got pregnant. A couple months after that Jess was killed.''

"That must have been hard on you,'' Garth said. "Being alone like that.''

"Having the baby alone was nearly unbearable. At least I thought it was. Then he was kidnapped and I thought I was going to die. But now I know that nothing can ever be worse than watching him suffer.''

Garth agreed but he knew that losing Amanda would run a close second. His sister's advice echoed in his head. Could theirs be a real marriage? After pondering that monumental question for several moments he thought of the more important one. The one on which the entire answer hinged, since Amanda's happiness was fast becoming one of Garth's main concerns. Was he capable of being what Amanda needed?

"I heard Jason say that you'd told him his father died a hero?" Garth asked, deciding that since she'd been happy with Jess Powers, he would be her measuring stick for a man. He might as well get some idea of what kind of man had made her happy. No telling where he'd fall when compared to a husband slain in the line of duty.

Amanda looked up from her needlework, a stunned look on her face. "What?"

"If it's still too painful for you to talk about him, I understand. Forget I mentioned it." He wasn't sure he really wanted to hear about Amanda's first husband.

"Painful?" She smiled. "Jess died over seven years ago, Garth. It isn't painful to talk about him. But it is pointless. Yes, Jess was a hero. Whatever that means. He died being a hero. To me that means he died and never saw his son born—never got a chance to be a father. I never cared about the accolades Jess received. They didn't make him a good husband. They didn't bring him back."

"Was he a good husband?" The answer could hurt, but he had to know.

Amanda raised an eyebrow as if it were something she'd never thought of. "A good husband? Jess never did anything by half measure so I guess that's what he tried to be. I was the envy of a lot of police wives because Jess didn't drink and he'd never have looked at another woman. He never brought the tensions of his work home, either. Jess saw the world in black and white—good or evil. Jason reminds me a lot of him in those ways.''

Garth had to wonder if there was any hope for him at all. He was far from the paragon she'd described. "It sounds as if he was perfect," Garth commented.

"No one is perfect, least of all Jess. We had good times and bad. Just like every married couple.''

Garth saw a glimmer of hope. "You had differences of opinion about some issues?"

Amanda nodded. "And he was killed before we were able to resolve them. I told you *I* didn't care about the accolades but at the end they were all he *did* care about. He'd work a second shift and be so wrapped up in his police life that he'd forget all about me and never call. So there I'd sit, worrying all night that something had happened to him and he'd just have forgotten to call. As the years went on, he took more and more extra duty. He became obsessed. We grew very distant.''

One mystery solved, Garth thought. That was why she'd so easily believed he hadn't called the night he'd sat out that storm in the hills of West Virginia. She'd been furious with him and he couldn't help wondering if he'd gotten caught in some old unresolved anger she held toward Powers. "You sound angry with him. He didn't choose to die, Amanda.''

"But he didn't choose to live, either. He could have waited for backup that night. He didn't. His partner was crippled and he was killed because Jess insisted they move in before their backup arrived. Jess lived on the edge and he liked it that way. An adrenaline high, he called it. He died for nothing but

I'm not angry at him. I forgave his foolishness long ago."

"You sure took off on me that night you thought I hadn't called to let you know I was grounded at Mayport. Are you denying it had anything to do with Powers?"

"I said I forgave him. I didn't say I'd forgotten. You never forget. It felt like the same thing all over again, is all."

"You seem like an unlikely pair," Garth commented, hoping to understand what had attracted her to Powers now that he knew something about him. Hoping knowledge of her past would give him some key to how to win her for his future. If indeed he did decide to try winning her. He was still not convinced he could be what she needed.

Amanda nodded. "He was always a little wild but basically he was a good man. Then my parents died in a boating accident. Jess was there, urging me to go away with him. Telling me he wanted me." She hesitated. "He was an experienced twenty-two to my very naive eighteen."

"Are you saying he pressured you to marry him?" Garth asked.

"I—I...in a way I suppose you could say that. And I'm sure he isn't the first or last man to go after what he wanted any way he could get results. He was going away from everything familiar and he wanted me to go with him. I really do believe he loved me. I just wish I didn't feel he manipulated me to get what he wanted." The pain and disappointment she swore she no longer felt was there for anyone to see or hear.

"We were young. I was suddenly alone. I loved Jess and he was leaving. He used every weapon in his arsenal to make sure I went with him. He even professed faith in Jesus, and I believed him even though my pastor didn't.''

"And that's the real issue for you, isn't it?"

"If the Lord had been foremost in his heart, getting medals and his name in the papers wouldn't have been important enough to risk his life for," Amanda said.

Garth stared into space, declining to make a comment. Jess Powers had hurt Amanda, that was for sure. He'd thought he needed to be more like Powers when the opposite was the case. Now he could see it. His similarity to Powers stood in his way, not his failure to measure up to the man.

And there was nothing he could do about it. Amanda was lost to him.

Because while his career was no longer the center of his existence, her Lord would never be either.

Chapter Nine

"Okay, troops," Garth said as he picked up the box of games and toys Jason had accumulated over his long hospital stay. "Do we have everything?"

Chris hefted the two plants she'd been assigned to carry. "Check," she called with a wide smile and headed for the door.

His mother held up her load—a suitcase in one hand and a fistful of strings that were attached to a dozen colorful balloons in the other.

"Check," she said and followed her daughter out of the room.

"Looks like everything to me," Amanda said and tucked a huge stuffed dog under one arm and an oversize Easter bunny under the other and marched out the door after his mother and Chris.

"Hey," Jason protested. "Didn't you guys forget somebody?"

Garth frowned. He looked around the bed and in the closet. "Now, let's see. Games and toys. Suitcase. Balloons. Plants. Stuffed animals. No. I don't think we forgot anything.''

"You forgot some*body*. Me!'' Jason squealed and hopped to his knees on the bed, his bright, ready smile proof that through his illness and the long months of isolation, Jason had retained his wonderful sense of humor.

Garth widened his eyes. "Well I think you're right, kiddo! You were supposed to come home with us today, weren't you? Do you think you could hang around another day? We've all got our hands full here.''

"No way. I'm going home. We're havin' a party.''

Garth laughed and held the door open so Maria Hernandez could push a wheelchair into the room. "Is this rotten father of yours pulling your leg?'' Maria asked.

Jason plopped his cap on his head, his lower lip pouted out. "Yeah.''

Maria planted her hands on her narrow hips. "Don't worry,'' she told Jason in a stage whisper. Then to Garth in a formal tone that was totally un-Marialike she said, "I'm afraid he'll have to leave today, Mr. Jorgensen. We need this room for someone who's really sick.''

"And I'm all better.'' Jason's eyes glowed with increasing strength and vitality. He slid off the bed and jumped into the wheelchair. "I'm outta here,'' he called over his shoulder as Maria pushed him toward the door and his future.

"Yeah,'' Garth whispered past the lump in his throat as he looked around the now empty room that had been all their home away from home for too long. "We're all outta here."

After lunch Garth swung Jason up onto his shoulders and carried him to his room. He'd talked Jason into resting on top of the covers. It was a compromise they'd reached when Jason was two and a half. The rest usually translated itself into a two hour nap. Garth had learned quickly that *nap* was a word to be avoided at all costs.

Once inside the room, he plopped Jason on the royal blue comforter that covered the top bunk. "Let's lose the shoes, shall we?"

Jason looked ready to argue on principle but nodded with a grimace. "Good idea. They're too small anyway. Could I have a pair of those really rad high-tops? You know the ones that have heels that light up when you walk?"

"Yeah, sure. Maybe we'll go to the shoe store tomorrow." Garth was so happy that Jason's feet had grown, a sign as far as he was concerned that his son was getting better, that he'd have agreed to gold-plated combat boots.

Jason stabbed his fist into the air. "Yesss!"

"But for now, you settle down," Garth ordered. "You know the drill. You don't have to sleep. You just have to rest."

In the hall, Garth nearly bumped into Amanda who'd been watching from the doorway. He saw the longing in her eyes and made a mental note to step aside that night so she could put her son to bed for the first time.

Amanda made an effort to look stern but her smile

blossomed as warm as ever. "You should be ashamed of tricking him that way. He won't be awake for five minutes and you know it."

Garth chuckled. "How do you think I survived all those years when he needed naps? If he didn't sleep when he was an infant, he sure didn't when he was two or three or four, either. I see parenting as sort of survival of the smartest and that kid would give a rocket scientist a run for his money. By the time he was three, I considered taking up ballet to help me keep on my toes."

"From the sounds of it, he's outsmarted you on many an occasion."

Garth dropped his arm around Amanda's shoulders and led her toward the stairs to the first floor. He could hear his mother and sister talking in the kitchen beyond. He felt guilty but he wished they weren't there. He'd held back for so long. Been careful to keep his distance except for small gestures for so long. He didn't know how much longer he could wait. "Hey, I'm not the only one he's gotten the best of. Ever hear the one about Smokie, the neighbor's cat and the day Jason decided he needed a bath?"

Amanda laughed and, as always, it did something to Garth. It flipped a switch. One position of that switch was labeled Father—the second was labeled Healthy, Needy Husband. Garth stopped in his tracks, halting Amanda's progress down the hall. He took a deep breath.

He'd spent the months of their marriage trying to keep his hands off her, trying to respect their agreement for a platonic relationship. He'd spent a lot of time trying to get to know Amanda. Trying to learn what she wanted from life.

He had decided to put an all-out effort into building the kind of relationship between them that would make a woman like Amanda happy. He was fairly confident he could succeed. Hadn't he succeeded at everything in his life with the exception of marriage to Karen? And marriage to Amanda would be nothing like those nightmare days. It would be worth all the effort because he could no longer conceive of life without her.

He had buried his true feelings behind a facade of friendship. But his resolve had worn thin over time and now he was afraid it was gone. He wanted Amanda. He wanted her for his wife. His real wife.

He looked down into her sparkling, violet eyes as she looked up at him. Then they turned warm and inviting and a ragged sigh escaped her lips. Garth lifted a hand to her hair. She wore it pulled away from her face in a braided arrangement that made her look about seventeen and made him feel like an adolescent again.

"You're so beautiful," he whispered against the delicate shell of her ear. He tugged her closer and tilted her face to his. Garth hadn't kissed her in so long. He'd been so very careful but he knew if he didn't kiss her right then, he'd lose his mind.

He'd already lost his heart.

Garth watched her eyes soften as he lowered his head toward hers. He'd been afraid she might pull away but he'd steeled himself for disappointment for no reason. Instead, she melted against him and reached up to sift her fingers through his hair. Her touch felt so right. "Amanda, I—" He shook his head unable to say more. He decided to let his kiss do his talking for him.

Amanda's lips under his made Garth think of tomorrows. Possibilities. A future with her in it. He had come to need Amanda in his life more than he needed air to breathe.

Then the voices of his mother and sister drifted up the stairs and shocked him back to reality. He would not seduce Amanda into making theirs a real marriage. She would have to settle for a man who could not share her faith. If Amanda decided to change their agreement it would be because she decided to— not because they'd consummated their marriage and she felt trapped.

He pulled back and put her away from him. "I'm sorry," he said, furious with his own weakness. "This isn't part of the bargain."

Amanda's violet eyes suddenly blazed. He'd never seen her so angry. "Then keep your hands to yourself!" she said through gritted teeth, her Southern accent suddenly thick enough to cut with a knife. "And let me tell you one more thing, Mister Jorgensen! If you apologize to me one more time for kissin' me, I'll clobber you. When I want an apology, I'll ask for it. Excuse me. Our guests are doin' the lunch dishes."

Amanda waited in Jason's room for Garth to help him finish his bath. She was anxious to tuck him into his own bed for the first time. It was another precious first Garth had given her and she loved him for suggesting it. It was tough staying angry at someone who was so considerate.

The problem was that Garth was too considerate at times. Like earlier that day in the hall. How on earth was she supposed to make this marriage last a lifetime when he continued to apologize for every kiss? Each apology served as a reminder that, to Garth, theirs was a temporary union. She couldn't help but feel rejected and the pain of those rejections increased with each passing day.

She sighed and looked around Jason's room. It spoke of budding masculinity, intelligence and creativity. Jason seemed to have participated in nearly every sport organized for boys. On one wall hung a collage of sports equipment, only some pieces of which she recognized.

He had a set of drums in one corner and a computer station in another. Jason was into the computer age in a big way. He was also a consummate Trekkie. The latter interest seemed to have inspired the scheme for decorating the entire room. It looked like a child's bedroom right off the *Enterprise*.

She chuckled, remembering the days he and Garth spent killing time in the hospital. Over the past three months, they'd built models of every starship ever conceived from the first *Enterprise* to *Voyager*. Her heart swelled at the memory of Garth's and Jason's heads bent close together in serious conference over a mock-up of the far wall of Jason's room.

She walked over and set one of those carefully constructed models into a swaying motion. Last week she'd helped Garth suspend the starships on fishing line from the ceiling in front of a wall mural of the Milky Way galaxy, which took up the whole wall.

It was a room that had been decorated with loving hands. The furniture had a space-age quality, the bunks built of bright red metal tubing. The white Formica bureau and desk, with their bright royal blue drawers and red knobs, looked indestructible. Garth had even found a deep blue carpet scattered with stars that he had matched in the ceiling. The stars on the ceiling glowed in the dark.

Amanda picked up Jason's discarded sweat suit and went to the closet to hang it up. She laughed when she slid the pocket door open. The closet walls always tickled her. They were the same deep matte blue as the bedroom ceiling but a grid work of white tape had been applied over it.

"You still think it's funny but you wouldn't laugh if it had been you," Garth growled in her ear, amusement showing through his gruff tone. "I almost went cross-eyed doing that."

Amanda turned. "What would a 'Star Trek' room be without its own holo suite?" she asked.

Garth rolled his eyes. "You're as bad as Jason. Now I know where it comes from."

"So, how come you went to so much trouble for a closet?"

"I figured he'd keep it neat if he wanted to show it off and I had extra paint."

"Mom, isn't that the coolest closet?" Jason said as he came into his room all fresh from his bath. "Dad didn't want to do it but I won so he was stuck."

Amanda lost a short battle with a grin when she

glanced at Garth who winced. "Extra paint, huh? What did you win?" she asked her son but kept her eyes on Garth.

"*Interloper.* It's a video game. Want me to show you how to play it?" Jason asked.

"Get the gleam out of your eyes, son. There's plenty of time for video games tomorrow. Right now you need to get some sleep. Now come here and give me a big hug and kiss. Then I'll see you in the morning. Mom's going to read to you tonight."

Jason dove into Garth's arms and was wrapped in a bear hug as Garth scooped him up. "You're not working tomorrow, are you?" he asked Garth.

"Not tomorrow but the next day, son. That temporary pilot left last week. I've got to get back to working my regular schedule. Money doesn't grow on trees, you know."

"But I thought we could take Mom to see Philadelphia. She's never seen the historical sights or the Franklin Institute. We should take her to the art museum and the zoo, too!" Jason squealed and bobbed up and down in Garth's arms. "And maybe Adventure Park. It'll be open on the weekends soon."

"We'll see. Don't forget you have schoolwork to catch up on and I'll still have office work to handle besides my flight hours. We'll fit in what we can. Okay?"

"Sure," Jason answered, only a little disappointment showing in his tone. "Will my tutor start coming again soon, too? She's cool. Not as cool as Mom but she's cool, you know?" Jason directed his attention toward Amanda. "Um, Mom, about breakfast. Do you think you could cook mine? I never had my own mom cook breakfast for me and that pizza you made for dinner was really awesome.''

"And while you're at it, could you make mine, too?'' Garth asked. There was the same little-boy hopefulness in his face as had been in Jason's. They looked so much alike that sometimes she forgot they weren't really father and son.

Amanda reached up and ruffled Jason's hair. "Grandmom and I already worked out the division of the housework. She has her jobs and I have mine.''

"You're going to be the cook I hope?'' Jason asked.

"Well, you see, sweetie, I hate doing dishes. Always have, so I was reluctant to take over the kitchen,'' she confessed with a twinkle in her eye.

Jason looked horrified. "But we'd help you. Wouldn't we, Dad?''

"Sure,'' Garth answered.

Amanda clapped her hands and smiled. "Wonderful! I'd *hoped* you'd both say that. Since I'm now chief cook, we'll all be the bottle washers.''

Garth chuckled. "I think we've been set up, kiddo.''

Jason sighed dramatically, then said dreamily, "Oh, I don't care. Won't it be great not to get waked up by a smoke detector?'' He levered upward in Garth's arms and whispered in his father's ear, then dove into the top bunk.

Garth laughed. "Me too, son,'' he said cryptically, kissed Jason, then left.

Amanda wondered about Garth's answer and Jason's secret question all the while she read Jason a story, heard his prayers and tucked him in.

"You too, what?" she asked Garth when she found him at the desk in his office.

Garth looked up from his papers with a roguish grin curving his lips. He rolled his leather armchair away from the desk and snagged her around the waist, pulling her close. He gave her a quick, smacking kiss. A kiss that he didn't apologize for. "I like you a lot better than his tutor. So does Jason. She was his last matchmaking effort before he met you." She squirmed away, profoundly confused by his vacillation from cold to affectionate.

"Should I be jealous?" she teased.

But Garth's eyes turned suddenly serious as they captured Amanda's. "No. I swore I'd never get married again. Until I met you, no one even tempted me."

"But you were forced into this marriage," Amanda countered.

Garth raised an eyebrow, still holding her gaze. "Was I?" he asked, then went back to reading the report on the desk. Amanda stared at his bent head wondering what was going on. It would take a lifetime to figure this man out. Shaking her head she turned and left.

Garth braked to a stop as the traffic came to a standstill once again. Amanda didn't care about the traffic jam. She was fascinated by the hustle and bustle of the city. The downtown area was a well-blended mixture of old and new. This was their first outing as a family that wasn't shopping or a movie. Amanda could scarcely contain her excitement.

"Do you and Jason go to the Franklin Institute often?" she asked Garth who was busy looking for a break in the traffic.

"Several times a year."

"What if Jason's bored?"

Garth reached out and put his hand over hers where it rested on her knee. "He's going to have a good time showing you all his favorite exhibits. They rotate special exhibits but others were here when my parents brought me. They have a lot of exhibits on technology. And Jason's crazy about technology," he added as the lane on their right cleared and he steered into it.

"Look, Mom. There's the art museum."

"I want to grab the first parking place I can so keep your eyes peeled for a spot you two."

"There, Dad. On that side street!"

"Way to go, kiddo," Garth said as he made a sharp right.

Garth watched Amanda as she played virtual reality volleyball with Jason. The silhouette of her figure was reflected on a tall wide screen. To him, she was perfection. Evidently several other men thought so, too. They all watched her with awe in their gazes. She wasn't very good at the game but she was something to watch all the same. The only trouble was he didn't want them looking. Amanda missed the "ball" one last time and let out an outraged cry as the screen went blank.

"Next group," the operator of the exhibit called

out. Amanda bent to pick up her purse and tripped into Garth's arms as she came upright. He smiled and held her longer than was necessary, neatly getting his message across to all the men who'd been watching her. She was his.

"Can we eat now?" Jason asked.

"Again?" Garth asked, teasing his son for the wonderfully voracious appetite that had come with his healing. Jason's color was healthy and he was beginning to outgrow his jeans. He even had a fuzz of dark hair on his head. Garth caught himself grinning. Life was good. In fact, today it was downright wonderful.

Amanda suggested a quick stop at one of the snack bars. Garth took the opportunity to indulge Amanda with her favorite new food—Philly soft pretzels with gobs of mustard. She gobbled hers even faster than Jason, then they went off to find the train. All three of them climbed all over the big engine. They investigated it thoroughly, teased each other and play-acted a train robbery until Jason grew bored. Garth jumped down, then reached up to swing Jason to the ground. But it was hard to see his son so full of energy and not give him a big hug. He usually resisted the impulse for Jason's sake but this time it was too great a temptation.

Amanda stood in the engine compartment and watched Garth hug Jason. She felt left out for a second, then fought off the stupid jealousy that still cropped up at odd moments. Jason couldn't have a better father and it wasn't Garth's fault that this was the first outing of this kind she'd ever had with her son.

Determined to join them, Amanda looked about in search of a way to the ground. As she took her first step out onto a piece of ironwork, her foot slipped. She gasped as her own weight pulled her hand loose and she lost her grip on the bar she'd held. Amanda knew a split second of terror as the hardwood floor rose up to meet her. But in the next heartbeat, she found herself cradled in strong arms and against a hard chest. Garth's chest.

Instinctively, Amanda wrapped her arms around his neck and found her gaze snared by his blue eyes. She thought the angels were surely proud of the color God had painted there. "Wedges of sunlight," she murmured as she stared, mesmerized by the golden flecks she'd never noticed before.

Garth, too, stared then gave his head a quick shake. "Are you okay?"

"Okay?" she asked, confused and still a bit disoriented by the fall but mostly by his nearness. "Oh! Yes. I'm fine." Did her voice sound as breathless to Garth as it did to her?

"You didn't hit your head on the engine when you slipped, did you?"

"No. Why?" she asked and cursed her still vague tone.

"You said something about wedges of sunlight. I thought you hit your head and were seeing stars or something."

"Your eyes have wedges of yellow in them. I never noticed."

"Oh. I guess I never did, either," he said, still not taking his eyes off her.

Then a little voice said, "You can put Mom down

now, Dad. Everybody's staring. She'll be careful from now on, won't you, Mom?''

Garth dropped her almost like the proverbial hot potato. One second she was cocooned in his embrace waiting for a kiss and the next she couldn't help but feel abandoned as she found her feet on the hard wooden floor. He backed away, his jaw rigid and his eyes blank of expression where seconds earlier they'd been open and achingly vulnerable. Or was that her overactive imagination? Or her hopeful heart?

''Jason wants to see the air travel exhibits next,'' Garth said taking two more steps backward.

Amanda refused to show him how empty his sudden desertion made her feel. ''Oh, good! Since you're a pilot you can explain to me what keeps those things in the air. I've never understood.''

Garth smiled, if a little stiffly and Amanda relaxed. At least he hadn't apologized for the near kiss. That was a bit of progress anyway.

''Come on, then. If these exhibits don't explain it to you, you'll never understand it.''

''I'll never understand it,'' Amanda said, throwing up her hands. Garth looked on with amusement as Jason once again manipulated the wing.

''But Mom don't you see—''

''I see the smoke going over the wing,'' she interrupted. ''It's lovely but it doesn't explain a thing. Where's the air come from?''

''Daaadd!'' Jason whined, ''she still doesn't get it. You try again.''

Garth held up his hands and not in mock surrender.

"Nope. I know when I'm licked. Might as well accept it, son. In aviation circles, she's what we call a hard case. I think it's time for the planetarium."

"Oh, yes. That sounds like a good idea," Amanda said.

"That's what you said about *this* exhibit," Jason chided.

Garth grinned at her, then scooped Jason up on to his shoulder. "Come on, kiddo. I think we've all had enough of the aviation world for one day."

Jason wilted dramatically against Garth. "More than enough."

"I'm not all that bad!" Amanda protested as she walked purposefully over to the hot-air balloon exhibit and pushed the button that started the burner. "I understand how this works. Heat the air and the air inside gets lighter—the balloon goes up. It cools off and it comes down. Simple. Airplanes weigh too much. They should drop like rocks. They're in a class with bumblebees as far as I'm concerned. They definitely should not be able to fly."

Garth sighed and shook his head. "A hard case, son. So, on to the planetarium? Jason can rest during the show."

"But I don't have to nap, right?" Jason asked his inevitable question.

Of course, Jason did nap and Garth was glad he'd sat their son between them. In a darkened movie theater with the stars above and a pair of amorous teens in front, having Amanda right next to him would have been more temptation than he could have resisted. He'd have kissed her within five minutes of the darkening of the lights. And he'd already almost kissed her long and hard in the middle of the institute earlier. That just wouldn't do. Because Amanda was worth the wait.

After the show, they visited the future exhibits and the one honoring historical accomplishments like the telegraph. Jason played for a while trying to master Morse code before they moved on to the scheduled paper exhibit.

"Where shall we eat?" Amanda asked when the demonstration drew to a close.

"I've got a picnic basket in the car," Garth said. "Suppose we go over into the park, eat, then come back in?"

Jason looked dubious. "A picnic basket that Mom doesn't know about? Dad, you didn't let Grand-mom—"

Garth chuckled. "Do I look like a fool? *I* packed it."

Jason grimaced. "Dad, you cook as bad as Grand-mom."

"But I know I can't cook! Oh, ye of little faith! Wait until you see the feast I bought when I went out to gas up the car this morning."

"Good, because I'm starved. Jason is, too!" Amanda said.

Garth loped ahead of Amanda and Jason. He went to the car, picked up the insulated basket, blanket and bag of toys he'd brought, then he went to meet them in the park across the street from the institute. Since it was a weekday and school was in session, the park was nearly empty. He spread the blanket out in the sun while Amanda listened to Jason's discourse on flying once again. He chuckled at Jason's exasperation when she still didn't get it.

"Chow time," he called out, changing the subject.

"What did you buy?" Amanda asked.

"Sit," he ordered and pulled her down next to him. The gourmet deli not far from their house specialized in box lunches. He took out the plastic boxes and handed them around. "Ham and cheese on white with crusts trimmed, potato salad and a sweet pickle for Jason."

"Way to go, Dad! My favorite. What do I get to drink?"

"A Ben's Berry-Berry Cooler." He felt in the basket. "And it's still cold. A turkey on a sourdough roll with diet mayo and lettuce with a tossed salad for a certain Mrs. Jorgensen."

Amanda chuckled at Jason who was tearing into his lunch. "Thank you. My favorite. And what do I get to drink?"

Garth grinned and pulled out a thermos. "Iced tea for the adults. Jason and I have almost the same lunch except I eat my crusts."

Amanda grinned up at him. "Good boy." She yanked on the dark curl that always fell over his forehead. "Crusts make your hair curl. My nana said so."

Garth traced her abundant waves. "What did you have to eat for these?"

"Hmm. Let's see. Carrots for my good eyes. Crust for curls. I remember. Potato skins!"

"Potato skins? Mom, your nana was as nuts as Grandmom."

"Jason, that wasn't kind," Garth admonished.

"Your grandmother is older and she has a few..." Words failed him.

"Eccentricities?" Amanda supplied, fighting a grin.

"What's that mean?"

Now Garth was fighting a grin. "It means that when you're seventy, you can say what you want and pip-squeaks like you aren't allowed to poke fun."

Jason looked at his plate. "I'm sorry."

"It's okay, pal. I know there are a lot of rules but your mom and I are here to teach them to you. No one's mad. I just want you to treat people with respect."

Jason nodded.

"Are you going to eat that salad or just play with it?" Garth asked his son after a few minutes of silence.

Both he and Amanda went off into gales of laughter over the way Jason hugged his plate to him and quickly took a big mouthful of salad. But later, when he put his head down and drifted off for one of his rests that were definitely not naps, they watched in contented silence until a backfire from a truck woke their son and he was once again raring to go.

Chapter Ten

"Come in," Amanda called and glanced up as her secretary, Julie, appeared in the doorway. In her hands was a crystal vase of white roses with sprigs of baby's breath and airy ferns intermixed in the bouquet.

"Flowers," the young woman sang out, a bright smile gleaming in her face.

Amanda felt her heart pick up its beat as it always did when Garth made one of these gestures. "My goodness! Again!"

"Your husband certainly didn't spare any expense this time."

Amanda stood and rounded the desk to take the vase. She took a deep breath. "The whole room smells like a rose garden."

"That's because your Garth sent you the whole rose garden. Two dozen! I counted. What's the excuse this time?"

Amanda set the bouquet on the credenza behind

her desk and plucked the card from its center. "Thanks for waiting up for me. The dinner, even three hours late, was the best. G."

"He was late last night. I waited up and kept his dinner warm," Amanda explained.

"Woooeee, that man's crazy about you," Julie declared.

"He's just grateful," Amanda said suddenly downhearted. Lately she and Garth were like ships passing in the night, or the morning depending on his flight schedule. She didn't see enough of Jason, either, for that matter.

Though she had a good position at a large insurance company, it wasn't as fulfilling as she knew staying at home would be. She wanted to be Jason's mother and Garth's wife, not the head of the actuarial department. But if Garth went ahead with the divorce, she'd need to support herself and Jason.

"Why so glum all of a sudden?" the young woman asked. "I wish that man of mine would send me flowers once in a while."

Amanda shrugged. No one but Garth's family knew about their arrangement. Sometimes she longed for a listening post. And Julie might just be the perfect person. Wise beyond her years and a devout Christian, her secretary might just have been sent by the Lord as a friend.

"I miss him," Amanda admitted. "We see so little of each other with me working. Garth has an erratic schedule. Sometimes he flies at night. If I'm here during the day, when are we supposed to build a marriage?"

Julie stared. "Build a marriage? Woman, you've

got yourself a great marriage." Amanda didn't respond but just stared at the flowers. "Don't you?"

"I don't know what I've got, Julie." Amanda bit her lip trying to keep the tears at bay. "I'm so confused."

"Back in a sec," Julie said, then turned and walked out of the office, returning minutes later with two cups of coffee in her hands. She kicked the door shut on her way past. "Let's take a break and have a little girl talk, shall we? You look like you could use it. Sit and talk, girl!" she ordered.

Amanda obediently sat back down at her desk as Julie took the chair in front it. "Garth didn't want to marry me," Amanda began. "At least I don't think he did. And I didn't want to marry him but I had no choice. At least I don't think I did. So you see, I'm not sure what I have."

Now Julie looked as confused as Amanda felt. "Start from the beginning, okay?"

Amanda did, pouring out the whole story starting with meeting Jess at fifteen up to the present. She was surprised that so many years condensed into so few words. Then Amanda realized how little living she'd done in the years her son had been missing.

"Why are you here?" Julie asked.

"Here? In Philadelphia?"

"In this office," Julie replied. "Amanda, your life isn't here. You need to be with your family, as you said, building a marriage. Don't get me wrong. I'm not one of these people who think a woman can't have a career and a successful marriage. That's the calling the Lord has given some women. Good as you are at your job, this isn't your calling. I've seen you with decorating magazines, poring over the pages for ideas. Have you put even one of those ideas into effect?''

''No. Garth made it very clear that the house was his. He even wanted a prenuptial agreement.''

''Yeah, but that was in case of divorce. You aren't going to get divorced. That man's crazy about you.'' She tapped her chin. ''But something's holding him back. What you've got to do is show him how good having you around is. And the only way to do that is to *be* around. Go home and make it your home, Amanda. Put your stamp on it.''

''It sounds like it could be a good plan.''

''You've got everything to gain by trying it. I'm sure going to miss you around here, girl.''

Amanda laughed. ''You've hardly had time to get used to having me here. You're saying I should quit?''

''Can Garth support you? Is your policy your family's medical insurance or can you go on his plan?''

''I guess so. I could have put Garth on my plan when we got married but I forgot all about it with Jason so sick. Jason!'' Amanda smacked herself on the forehead. She couldn't believe she'd forgotten something so important! ''I've always carried Jason on my insurance because I wasn't sure what kind of condition he'd be in when I got him back. My insurance should have picked up Jason's bills all along. I imagine they still can. Garth's pretty tight financially right now because of all the medical bills. He said he had to take out a second mortgage on the house and on Liberty Express, too. It would help him so much to get that money back. It'll probably be a real tangle but I think they have to pay.''

''You better get that all squared away before you even consider quitting. You don't need your salary, do you? I don't want to advise you to quit work if you can't afford it.''

''No. It just goes in the bank. I wanted to contribute but Garth doesn't want me to spend it except for my expenses. I imagine that's because he knows he won't be supporting me or Jason after the divorce.''

''But there isn't going to be a divorce,'' Julie corrected. ''Keep telling yourself that. Continue on as if you never heard the word. Make plans just as if you never agreed to it. Go home tonight and show that man what he'd be missing if he let you get away.''

''You really think being at home might help?''

''Pray about it and in the meantime talk to personnel about this insurance thing.'' She pointed to the flowers and smiled widely. ''A little gratitude got you them. No telling what getting his business and house out of hock might get you.''

''It's a big step. This job means financial security for Jason.''

''Like I said, pray about it, Amanda. Then give notice if the Lord confirms it in your heart. I just know He wants Garth as your husband.''

Garth picked up the envelope and stared at it. He had a ton like it in the drawer. The return address read Children's Hospital of the University of Pennsylvania. ''Another bill,'' he said, with a sigh. Suddenly, though he'd just gotten up, Garth felt exhausted. He even toyed with the idea of adding it unopened to the others in the drawer. Why did he want to know how much more money he owed?

Selling Liberty had already begun to look like the best solution. His only acceptable solution. Declaring medical bankruptcy was not an option. He would provide for his family. He had to!

Headhunters representing three different major carriers had called in the last month looking to fill empty slots. He had promised jobs waiting with two of them and had already flown as a fill-in pilot for one of them—his old airline—last week. And the money from the sale would just about pay off every last one of the bills that had been piling up. He looked again at the offending envelope. It would have until today, that was.

Selling sounded so easy except that he didn't want to sell. Amanda had asked him to wait. And he had. But he couldn't stall much longer. Potential buyers didn't wait forever.

Garth turned the envelope over in his hand. Something told him to tear it open so he did. And he just stared. It was a check. Not a bill. A check. Credit for payments made in error it said. A hundred thousand dollars. About five thousand more than the second mortgages on the house and Liberty Express.

What in the world was going on in the hospital accounting office? If he wasn't an honest man, he'd run right out and pay off the mountain of debt burying him. Instead, shaking his head over the monumental errors made by today's whiz-bang computers, Garth picked up the phone and dialed the hospital.

Ten minutes later he hung up and sat, staring at

the check. His check. Not one printed in error. Amanda had seen to it that she was now to be considered the primary person responsible for Jason's bills. Garth could feel his pulse beating in his temple. Did she think him incapable of supporting her and her son? Had he ever given her any indication that he needed her money?

His father's strident tones rang in his ears, conjured up from deep-seated memories. *A pilot? Where do you think you'll learn to be a pilot? What kind of an occupation is that? You'll never support a family with that kind of pie-in-the-sky dreaming. Get your head out of the clouds, boy.* But Garth hadn't been able to and he'd hated himself for having foolish dreams. Then pleasing his unpleasable father had no longer mattered. So he'd gone to his congressman and before he'd known it his dreams were happening. He was an officer in the United States Air Force and headed for top gun school. And he could support a family very well, thank you.

Garth didn't want to think about Amanda's motives. He just wanted to let her know what he thought of her lack of faith in him. He picked up the phone and dialed her at work.

"Actuarial department—"

"Amanda Jorgensen," he snapped and grimaced, realizing that he'd taken out his anger on Julie, Amanda's friendly, young secretary.

"Hi," Amanda said, her voice annoyingly cheerful.

"It's Garth. I'd like to talk to you if you have a minute."

"What's wrong? You sound upset."

Garth could barely speak he was so angry but he managed. "Did you change Jason's records to make you responsible financially for his medical care?"

"Well, technically—"

"Yes or no!" Garth demanded between clenched teeth.

"Yes," Amanda said, sounding confused and annoyingly innocent. "It was the only way to straighten out the mess. Red tape at—"

"Have I ever given you any indication that I am unable or unwilling to provide for you and Jason?"

"That wasn't the issue. Jason is my son and therefore—"

"He's my son, too. You've said so often enough. He took sick while in my care. I am perfectly capable of paying for his medical expenses."

"I never said you weren't. But—"

"But nothing! I'll leave the hospital's refund on your dresser. I don't pretend to know where you got all that money but you can just put it back in whatever account it came from." Not caring to hear empty platitudes about his financial reversals or the extraordinary number of expenses he'd incurred because of Jason, Garth hung up.

Amanda sat staring at the phone in stunned silence. What on earth had just happened? Why did nothing she did where Garth was concerned go right!

"Did the phone self-destruct after I connected you?"

"Was he rude to you?" Amanda asked, shocked that Garth would take his anger out on someone innocent of any wrongdoing. Wait a minute. What was she thinking? She was innocent, too!

Julie waved a careless hand in the air as she sat across from Amanda. "Don't worry. He just growled your name. So, what did you do to put the thorn in the lion's paw?"

"A cardinal sin. I claimed against my health insurance for all of Jason's expenses and got a bundle of money returned to Garth. Clearly, I should be taken out and stoned!"

"Now calm down and let me get this straight, girl. You went ahead and got his house and business out of hock and he's *angry?*"

Amanda nodded. She didn't know what to feel. Hurt? Anger? Her anger had already ebbed away. Right now she was numb. But hurt was nibbling away at it. Get angry again, she told herself. It hurts less.

"The way I see it, your man has a real problem where money's concerned. And you could react two ways. I don't think handing him his head would be very constructive, however satisfactory."

"Right about now it sounds like a pretty good idea to me."

"Or you could call his mother and ask her why she thinks Garth reacted to good news so badly. Could be that the answer might just drain all that anger away. Then you could let Garth know that even though you understand why he acted the way he did, he hurt you. Make him grovel around for forgiveness. It's better than a good scream any day."

Amanda laughed. "Julie, you are a godsend."

"Yeah. Yeah. That's what they all say. Then they give notice and go on their merry way, leaving poor Julie to train another boss."

"I think I'll call and talk to my mother-in-law. She may know what this is all about."

Amanda walked up the front path a bit earlier than usual that night. She couldn't put off the coming confrontation any longer. Frieda met her at the door.

"I sent Jason over to a friend's to play. I didn't want him upset. Garth's barely been civil all day. Try to remember that he acts like this when he's hurt."

"Julie's lion with a thorn in his paw." Amanda smiled. "I'm in good company anyway. I'm not the first Christian to confront a lion. Where is he, anyway?"

Frieda grimaced then chuckled. "In his den."

Amanda snickered. "We shouldn't be laughing. This is serious."

"Of course it is. Don't you spare his feelings. I heard the volume he used when he called you this morning. He deserves to eat some crow." The older woman chuckled again. "Do lions eat fowl?"

Garth looked up as Amanda walked into his study. She hadn't bothered to knock. "We need to talk, Garth," she said as she plunked herself down in the chair across from him.

"The check's on your dresser. I don't want to discuss it further."

"You prideful fool! That money represents all you've paid so far that is *now* paid by my insurance. I've carried health coverage on Jason since he was born. Why shouldn't I claim against it? Jason is your son by virtue of your love for him and his for you, but I gave birth to him. I can't see the harm in using the insurance I paid for for years! My policy predates yours, so I had to be the one on record as being chiefly responsible. Your policy picked up the rest. Much of what you paid had to be returned.''

Garth had a sinking feeling in the pit of his stomach. He'd made a complete fool of himself. ''Insurance?''

''In-*surance!*'' Light suddenly dawned in Amanda's eyes. ''Good heavens! You thought I sent them a check? Where would I get that kind of money?''

''Life insurance on your husband. Wise investments. I don't know. Why didn't you tell me about this?'' Garth asked, raking a hand through his hair.

''Because no one told me it had been settled. I didn't want to get your hopes up once I found out how much money was still outstanding on Jason's account, so I decided to wait and tell you when I was sure both coverages would pay for everything. These things usually take time but because I'm an employee, personnel promised to speed up the process. I guess they forgot to tell me it had all been worked out.''

Garth took a deep breath. ''Amanda, I'm so sorry. I acted like an idiot.'' He spread his hands in a gesture of helplessness. ''I don't know what else to say.''

Amanda fixed him with a long, level stare. ''You can start by telling me where all that anger came from. I think you owe me that much.''

Her request shocked him. Especially since he didn't know why he'd gotten so angry. It was all tied up with Jason. Money.

And Amanda's opinion of him. He'd thought that he'd failed her at the most basic of levels. That she didn't trust him to provide for her and Jason. That she saw him as a foolish dreamer...just the way his father had. But that was ridiculous! His father was dead and buried. He had no effect on Garth's life at all. Did he?

Not one to lie to himself once he stared the truth in the face, Garth admitted that it had been his father's berating voice he'd heard in his thoughts just before making the call to Amanda. Now he really felt like an idiot. How could he admit that to Amanda? The woman he wanted to share his life with. The woman he'd been trying to woo for months into remaining his wife. Well, if he didn't want all that work to go to waste he'd better think of something to explain his outburst—or admit to the truth.

Garth sighed. Painful as it was, the truth was his only option. He would not lie to Amanda. "Did you ever have a dream? One that was so far above the realm of possibility that it seemed almost unattainable?"

"Going to Tulane," Amanda said. "But I worked hard at the local community college. Then I got a grant because my parents were killed and Jess offered to pay the rest."

"Did you have the dream before your parents died?"

"They told me to work my hardest, pray for it and trust in the Lord."

"That's pretty much what Mom told me. My father, on the other hand, called me a fool chasing a pie-in-the-sky dream—among other things. I was going to be a failure as a man and be unable to support my family.''

''And it seemed to you that I was saying the same thing?''

''Stupid, huh?''

Amanda shook her head. ''Not stupid. Garth, I understand that supporting your family is important to you. But do me a favor. Ask yourself if succeeding to the level you have would have been as important to you if your father had been like your mother. If he'd supported your dream. I'll just bet you never had to do anything to earn her love and respect.''

''No, Mom's always been there for both Chris and me. She never criticized us unless it was constructive. I guess maybe I'd be a little more relaxed about succeeding if he'd been like her. But he wasn't, Mandy. He tore us down at every opportunity. If I made a hit in a Little League game, it would have been a home run if I'd just hit the ball a little harder.''

Garth could feel the old anger and resentment begin to burn inside him. His hands seemed to ball into fists of their own accord. ''I remember getting an A on a really tough calculus test. He found it necessary to mention that it was a shame I missed the *easy* extra credit question. Not only did no one else get that extra credit question right, but my father couldn't do second-level algebra to save his life. He had no idea if that question was easy or not.''

''But you've proven him wrong,'' Amanda said and scooted to the edge of her chair so she could reach across the desk. She took his hand and uncurled it so it lay flat on the desktop. "You are what you said you'd be. How long are you going to let his memory do this to you, Garth? You need to forgive him and put the past behind you."

"I told you before, I'll never forgive him. Not for what he did to Mom or the way he treated Chris and me."

"Do you think your mother still goes through all these push-and-pull emotions where your father's concerned? She seems rather serene to me. She's put that part of her life behind her. She's able to live in the present and for the future. I don't think you can make that claim, can you? You're still the kid whose father didn't appreciate his test grade."

Garth stared at his hand, now flat on the desk and covered by hers. Emotions with no names warred in his heart and mind. "Until you pointed it out to me, I thought I'd gone beyond being that kid. But forgive him? I don't think I can. He hurt us all so badly."

"Do you have any idea how much energy it takes to hate someone the way you do your father? Your hatred makes you drive yourself harder than necessary. I know my situation with Jess wasn't the same but I had to come to a place where I forgave him."

"I've never understood how Mom was able to make her peace with my father."

"Why not ask her?"

Garth nodded, still staring at her soft hand. He was so ashamed of the way he'd acted. Maybe he would talk to his mother about that last meeting with his father. Amanda deserved so much better than a man like him. He'd just have to try harder. He had to make sure he never flew off the handle like that again. He had to make Amanda happy—had to be the man she needed him to be because there was no longer any chance that he could just let her go.

He looked up not knowing what to expect and found her smiling at him. "Now I have my own apology to deliver," she said. "I'm sorry I didn't tell you what I'd set in motion at work."

"Your apology is unnecessary, Amanda. I overreacted."

"Yes, you did but your overreaction doesn't negate my mistake. A marriage is a partnership. Partnerships don't function well if both parties act independently." She took a deep breath and rushed on. "So, before we have another misunderstanding, I remembered about the health insurance on Jason when I was talking to Julie about quitting my position."

"Quitting?" Garth couldn't believe what he'd heard. "Your job? You want to quit? I thought you wanted to work."

Amanda shrugged. "So did I. But I don't. I want to stay home and be a wife and mother. I've missed so much of Jason's life already that every day I spend away from him drives me crazy. Plus, your mother isn't getting any younger. She deserves a chance to kick back and give up some of the responsibilities of running a house and caring for Jason. So, if you have no objection I'd like to give my notice. We can still carry the double health insurance for up to three years by paying the premiums, just to be on the safe side where Jason's health is concerned."

Garth was almost afraid to breathe. Had he heard right? Amanda believed in him? She'd begun to see their marriage as a marriage, not some bargain struck under duress? She was willing to trade her job—her financial security—to stay at home and take care of him and Jason?

He might be reading too much into her gesture, though. She had said she missed Jason. And it would be just like Amanda to worry as much as he did that his elderly mother carried too much of a burden. He'd better not get his hopes up too much. Better to be practical. Safer, he decided.

But then an optimistic thought occurred to Garth and he hung on to it like a lifeline. When she'd mentioned continuing her health benefits, Amanda had said *we can still carry* which committed her to their marriage for at least three years. He had three years to show her how happy they could be together.

Chapter Eleven

Amanda gave her notice the next morning and, as Julie had predicted, was invited to return at any time. She prayed that returning to work was not part of her future. Insurance had never been her plan for the future anyway.

The next two weeks seemed endless, especially since Garth's schedule was more crammed than usual. He'd explained that he'd taken on more work, hoping to keep himself in the black so he wouldn't have to sell Liberty. Though he didn't need the work, he felt he should honor the commitments. But consequently, Amanda felt more isolated from him than she ever had.

Then finally her first Monday at home dawned. Garth rushed off to work with the promise to be home for dinner and Jason's tutor arrived at nine. After seeing Jason settled with the woman in the den, Amanda returned to the kitchen for a cup of coffee with Frieda.

Glancing around the utilitarian kitchen, Amanda's thoughts turned to color and style. How she wished she could redecorate Garth's home! There was nothing really wrong with this room except that it was dated and a little dingy. The rest of the interior of the house, with the exception of Jason's room, needed help, too. The formal areas especially needed a major overhaul. Japanese minimalist, chrome and glass had their place but, in Amanda's humble opinion, it was not in a two-hundred-year-old colonial.

Not knowing exactly who had chosen the odd pairing nor how much of the current decoration Frieda had chosen, Amanda was reluctant to approach the subject. The last thing she wanted was to offend Garth or his mother. Amanda realized how little she really knew about Garth. She didn't even know how long he'd owned the house. She almost let the whole subject lie but once again Julie's words of wisdom flowed through her thoughts. *Go home and make it your home, Amanda. Put your stamp on it.*

"Frieda, how long has Garth owned this house?" Amanda asked before she could once again lose courage.

Frieda tapped her chin. "Well, let me see. I didn't move here until after Jason came to us. I think he bought it right after his marriage. Though I don't remember them doing much to fix it up for some time. Even so, the effort was rather piecemeal," she snorted in disdain. "Truth be told. Not all of the problems in that partnership were due to Karen's mental illness. Neither one of them slowed down their schedules long enough to work at a marriage."

"Then Garth and Karen didn't decorate it together?"

"No. As I remember it, Garth planned the outside work." Shaking her head she added, "And Karen handled the inside." Her tone provided Amanda all the encouragement she needed. Frieda didn't approve of her late daughter-in-law's taste, either. Amanda gave the kitchen another close look. It didn't fit with the rest of the house.

"Oh, not this room, dear. That one wasn't much for the kitchen. This is the way it was when Garth bought the place. I've thought about trying to do something around here for years but, to be honest, I just didn't know where to start. It seems like such a monumental task and I'm not as young as I used to be. Would you consider it?"

Amanda breathed a sigh of relief. "That's what I was trying to get around to asking. I really think this house cries out for something a little more suited to the period. So, you wouldn't mind it if I tried a few new things?"

"I wouldn't mind it if you called the Salvation Army and emptied the whole place." Frieda giggled like a schoolgirl, then wiggled her eyebrows. "In fact, that might not be such a bad idea."

Later that day over dinner Frieda brought up the subject with Garth. "Amanda mentioned the decor around here today."

Garth looked around. "What decor?" he asked, sounding genuinely confused.

Frieda chuckled. "Exactly her point. Tell Garth what you'd like to do, dear."

Leave it to Frieda to just blurt out a sensitive subject. Amanda took a deep breath. "Well, actually I didn't have any definite plans. Just sort of a general idea of suiting the decorating a little more closely with the architecture and period of the house." Remembering how proprietary he was about the house she added, "You wouldn't feel I was intruding, would you?"

"Intruding?" Garth asked, frowning. "Amanda, this is your home."

"But—" About to bring up his past attitude and the prenuptial agreement, Amanda stopped. Now, in front of Frieda and, of course, Jason, was not the time. "But it would mean more than paper, paint and carpets. The furniture's all wrong for what I had in mind."

"Good. I hate most of it anyway." He thought for a minute. "All of it actually, except for the stuff upstairs in my study."

"That furniture was from your apartment, wasn't it?" his mother asked, casting a determined look in Amanda's direction.

Garth nodded, so Amanda jumped in with a few suggestions to brighten up his private domain without changing its basic style. "You're probably more qualified to decide what it should look like than I am," Garth responded. "I'd kind of like to see what you can do with this old barn. I suppose you'll want to hire a decorator."

Amanda's stomach dropped. Was he saying he didn't think she could do it on her own? "I hadn't planned on it. Do you want me to? It's your decision, after all." *It's your house* she almost added.

"Karen did, but to tell you the truth, if this place is an example of what a decorator would do, I'd rather you go it alone."

Now her heart pounded. Not only did he not mind her changing his home but he trusted her to do it right. "It might get messy for a while."

"Not a problem." Garth grinned. "If I could live with that thing in the family room that's supposed to be my easy chair for all these years, I can live with anything. I'll give you my credit card. Get whatever you want."

"Don't you want to have some input into what I do?"

Garth stared at her for a moment, then shrugged. Sometimes she thought they must look like wary children, both afraid to say what they wanted, both afraid it was too much to ask. "Is that what you'd like? You wouldn't mind me looking over your shoulder?"

"I thought we could make some of the decisions together," she ventured, praying he'd want to work with her—as a real married couple would.

Garth smiled. A little dimple in his cheek appeared and his eyes sparkled. He suddenly looked ten years younger than when she'd first met him. "Just let me know where and when."

Amanda smiled, too, unable to look away from his beloved face. She felt a bond forming between them that hadn't been there before. *Please. Please, let this mean something!*

"Mom? Dad?" Jason's worried voice cut through the connection with Garth and they both turned toward their son. "I like my room. Don't you?"

"Oh, goodness. I wasn't thinking of changing a thing in there," Amanda declared. "Except maybe we could do something about the stash of books under that bed. Some rolling drawers maybe."

Jason sighed dramatically then his eyes lit. "I thought of something my room could use."

"Not if it has anything to do with white tape!" Garth exclaimed and poked Jason in the belly.

Jason giggled. "I thought maybe a dog bed next to mine."

"Why would you want a dog bed?" Amanda asked. "You don't have a dog." Light dawned when Garth snickered. "Oh, you'd like to change that as well?" She looked toward Garth, gauging his reaction. But Garth had turned his head toward his mother. Amanda followed his gaze.

"Well, don't everyone look at me!" Frieda exclaimed.

"If I remember," Garth said tapping his forehead, "you've been the stumbling block in the past."

"Now that Amanda's here, I have no objection. As long as I'm not the one who has to take care of it. Which is why I objected. I had to feed that mongrel of Garth and Christina's for years after they left. You two had the fun when you visited and all I ever got was nearly knocked down every time I gave him his bowl." She huffed and stood to clear the table then stopped, a thoughtful look crossing her face. "Well," she added with a fond smile, "at least *he* enjoyed my cooking."

"He sure did, Mom. He ate enough of it under the table," Garth said in a muttered aside as the door to the kitchen closed behind Frieda.

Jason hooted and Amanda gave them both a reproving look as she stood to collect some more dishes. "You are both incorrigible." Just inside the kitchen she stopped to reflect. Garth hadn't been offended by her interest in the house. In fact, he'd seemed pleased. She looked around the kitchen. She couldn't wait to get to work!

Over dessert, plans for a trip to the SPCA began to form. Amanda couldn't have been more pleased. They were beginning to look and feel like a real family.

"You're sure that's the one you want, son?" Garth asked, eyeing the puny puppy in Jason's arms. Jason, and frankly he, had always preferred bigger dogs, not ankle biters. This one would clearly never grow to be anything but ankle high.

"He's so friendly." Jason sighed as the little dog licked his face once again.

Garth had to give the mutt several points for personality if not looks or stature. A nondescript gray, his wiry fur stuck out at weird angles. This was one ugly dog.

"The shepherd pup looks real friendly," Garth said encouraging Jason not to discount one of the more obvious choices.

"But don't you see…almost anybody would want him. But this puppy…well…"

"Has problems," Garth supplied, being as kind as he could. Garth took the dog from Jason and held the squirming little body next to his chest. And his heart melted when the pup looked up at him, his tongue darting out to give Garth a big puppy kiss.

His left ear drooped while the right perked up at attention, his big, brown, puppy eyes full of canine admiration. "Hold still and stop with the kisses, buster. That's not going to get you anywhere with me," Garth lied, trying to maintain some decorum and his image as a tough guy for his son.

"Buster! What a great name, Dad!" Jason reached up and ruffled the dog's unruly fur. Garth's melted heart puddled somewhere in his chest. He even got to name him. Oh, how he'd wanted a dog when he'd been Jason's age. His chance had only come after his father had exited their lives. But Garth had left for the air force a little over a year later.

"And Mom did ask us to get one that's not too big," Jason added unnecessarily.

Garth was going nowhere without Buster. "And she did say not to get one with a pedigree because they're sometimes harder to train. He's sure not in that category. We'll take this one," Garth told the approaching attendant who looked instantly confused.

"That one? But we don't have any records on that one. We just found him in a box on the doorstep. Can't say I'm surprised. The note said he'd been a big disappointment. Runt of the litter. We're not even sure what he is." He chuckled. "Except a pretty ugly dog."

Offended on behalf of the newest member of the Jorgensen clan, Garth glared. "He's the one. It's him or none. Right, Jase?"

Jason's head bobbed as he jumped up and down. "Right on, Dad!"

Garth filled out what felt like more papers than he

had the last time he'd bought a car, then after purchasing a dog carrier, he and Jason started their trip home. They stopped on the way though, to buy everything an abandoned doggy needed to make him feel like a part of the family.

"Garth, what is it?"

"A puppy," Garth told Amanda, once again offended on Buster's behalf. Were he and Jason the only people who saw Buster's potential?

"Well, he is small. I—I did say to go for one on the small side. And he sure doesn't have a pedigree. Nope. No AKC papers attached to old...what did you say Jason's going to call him?"

"Jason decided on Buster."

"But Dad named him. Said something like, 'You're not going to get to me with all those kisses, buster.' And I said, 'Buster! Let's call him Buster.' And so his name's Buster. What a great doggy name! Did you see all the stuff Dad bought him? Squeaky toys and a bed for my room and that new stuff so he won't get fleas, and leather chewies so he won't want Grandmom's slippers. He's gonna be the best little dog anybody ever had. I'm going to take him outside and show him the dog igloo we got. It's kind of big for him but it's the smallest one they sold."

Amanda turned to Garth after watching Jason and his small gray shadow run out the back door. "Runt of the litter? Garth, they don't usually use that term unless they are expecting a certain size within a litter."

"That was what the note said that was left with him. Can you imagine abandoning him like that on the front steps. Out in the woods the way the SPCA is? He could have been hurt by a predator before anyone found him."

Amanda stepped up to him and put her hand in the middle of his chest. "You're just an old softy, aren't you? You heard that story and just had to take him in." She tiptoed and planted a smacking kiss on his cheek. "You're a nice man, Garth Jorgensen." She moved forward to give him another friendly kiss and Garth turned his head. Their lips met. And the small token offered became so much more.

To both of them.

Amanda dabbed the last touch of paint on the wall and climbed down from her high perch on the ten-foot ladder. She stepped back to admire her masterpiece. The border of ivy vine she'd stenciled on the soffit over the kitchen cabinets looked exactly the way she'd hoped it would.

This afternoon, when the kitchen set she'd bought arrived, the room would be complete. It still amazed her that rock maple had been hidden under the chipped paint on the cabinets. What some people did to wood! Now stripped of their color and hand rubbed to a smooth patina, the cabinets looked more like antique furniture. And it had cost next to nothing.

Amanda had saved a bundle by using sponged-on paint and joint compound to give a textured colonial look to the walls and by refinishing the existing cabinets. She'd also haunted area thrift shops, estate auctions and house sales looking for a trestle table and benches. She'd finally found them at a bargain price.

An older woman had sold her the set at a fraction of what Amanda knew it was worth because it was going to a family and not to some "snooty" antique dealer. Amanda loved the sound of that. Family.

Smoothing her hand over the polished granite countertop that had arrived and been installed that morning, Amanda smiled. Now here she'd splurged but it had been well worth it, as had the hand-hewn panel that matched the cabinets and disguised the modern look of the dishwasher and refrigerator. The other big-ticket item had been the professional stove that, because of its utilitarian design, lent itself to the antique flavor she'd given the room.

Garth had spent the week away on a long charter, ferrying a state senator around on a campaign tour of Pennsylvania. Amanda couldn't wait for his return. When he'd left, the kitchen had been a disaster with doorless cabinets, an exposed subfloor and several holes in the plaster. It had been the perfect place to begin training Buster but hardly looked promising as a redecorating job. And now all she had to do was clean up her paints and sweep the new slate gray tile floor.

"The men are here with the table and benches," Frieda called from the front of the house just as Amanda put the broom in the closet.

Three hours later, she placed an old jar with a bouquet of daisies on the table. She looked around in tired anticipation as Jason called out. "Mom! Come quick. I think there's something wrong with Buster's paws. They're all swollen and even bigger than they were last night."

"I'm in the kitchen," she called, not as concerned

as Jason. Amanda chuckled. Since Wednesday, three days after Garth took off and five days after the puppy had come home with the hearts of her men firmly in his grasp, Amanda had suspected that she hadn't gotten one of the things on her doggy wish list. Buster was not going to be a little dog. His paws, so small that everyone had believed he'd never reach knee high, had…flowered. Sneakered feet thudded and puppy nails clicked as the pair came bounding into the room.

Hunkering down, Amanda picked up the squirming little dog. "Now, let's see." She poked and prodded each little puppy paw. The puppy was all paws. "Jason, I think his paws are just fine. He's just growing but his paws are growing a lot faster than the rest of him. What this means is that Buster isn't going to be a little dog when he grows up the way everyone thought. He may have been taken away from his mother a bit too young and so he seemed as if he were destined to be a little dog, but he was just a very young puppy."

"How big?" Jason asked, clearly not disappointed by this new development, just curious.

She put her hand off the floor. "Big-big." It was an underestimation, she was sure.

"Wow!" He stood. "Hear that boy? You're not a runt after all. Let's go tell Grandmom."

"I'm sure she'll be thrilled," Amanda said as the two raced off to find more adventure together. The *beep-beep* of a horn drew her to the back door then as Garth hopped out of his car.

He looked up and smiled. That dimple she'd never really taken note of until recently peeked out. He tilted his head and said, "Should I come around front or is the kitchen safe to navigate these days?"

Amanda folded her arms and tried to look annoyed at his teasing. "And I said you were nice? I stand corrected. I'll have you know that the kitchen is completely safe," she said as he reached the house. "And finished," she added when Garth stopped in his tracks just inside the door.

"Amanda! This is incredible." Garth dropped his bag and walked to the cabinets. He caressed the rock maple then the granite counter. Then he turned to her.

Amanda wished she could read his mind. Did he understand that this had been a labor of love for her? She voiced her big worry. "Then you like it? It isn't too...I don't know...rustic?"

Garth shook his head. "I feel as if I just stepped into the pages of a magazine. The 'after' photograph. You were wasted in insurance, Amanda. You should have been a decorator."

A smile bloomed on her face. "Actually, that's what I started out wanting to be. Insurance was just a job I qualified for because my major was in business. I minored in art and courses I hoped would get me into decorating later. But...well it was too tough to get into it. Real bottom-level starting salaries." And Amanda had felt honor bound to find a good paying job. Jess had spent so much on her education that she'd grabbed at the first job she could find. It was supposed to have been temporary.

"How did you do all this in a week? You must have worked around the clock."

Amanda didn't dare address the subject of her

hours. "It took longer than a week if you think about it. The place was already torn apart when you left. Everything had been ordered. You helped me pick out the stove. The carpenter you called had the cabinet doors to finish so they'd match the refrigerator and dishwasher panels he was making for us. The floor was almost ready for the tile masons. All that prep work is the part that takes the time. It usually looks its worst just before it all comes together. That's where we were when you left."

Garth reached out and snagged her into his arms and hugged her tightly. Amanda's heart skipped several beats then picked up its usual, if quicker, rhythm. "Thank you," he whispered into her hair. "I never realized having a wife could be this wonderful."

Garth tiptoed into the kitchen and shut the door behind him. It was two in the morning. He didn't want to wake anyone else just because sleep was further away now than when he'd gone to bed at midnight. He opened the fridge and pulled out the carton of milk. As he shut the door, he couldn't resist running his hand over the wooden panel. Even in the dark the scope of Amanda's efforts overwhelmed him.

He turned and grabbed a glass out of the cabinet and once again his fingers caressed smooth wood as if he had no control whatever over his actions. Which was even more true now that he'd learned how much of the work Amanda had done herself. With loving hands. That's what showed the most. That she'd cared about the room. He closed his eyes. Hopefully that was a sign that she cared about the man standing in the room at the moment.

He took a swallow of the cool milk. Marriage. He had so much to learn. It was a partnership, Amanda had said. Tomorrow they were going to pick out some furniture. She'd insisted. And he was glad. In fact, like a kid, that was why he couldn't sleep. He wanted tomorrow to come—to be here now!—so he could be with her.

Amanda.

It seemed that nearly every waking moment this past week—*Oh, be truthful with yourself at least, Jorgensen, nearly every moment for months*—was filled with thoughts of her.

He hated the nights the most all. It was the one time she wasn't his. The one time of the day when he couldn't pretend that the gulf between them didn't exist. He wanted her. It was that simple and that complicated. It didn't matter if she was all made up and dressed in fashion magazine splendor or if her cheek was streaked with paint and her clothes were full of it. He loved her and wanted to show her how much since the words seemed forever stuck in his throat.

"Garth? Son, is that you rattling around out here?"

Garth chuckled. "It better be or you have a milk-drinking burglar in your kitchen."

Frieda chuckled, too, and flipped on the under counter lighting. "Not my kitchen any longer." Frieda looked around. "It's Amanda's. She made it hers. She's a wonderful wife to you, son. Don't be a fool and lose her."

"I'm trying not to, Mom." Garth sighed and ran his fingers through his hair. "But you should know that sometimes marriages don't work out. I'm working as hard as I can but—"

"Work? Is that what you think Amanda deserves?"

"Marriages take work."

Frieda reached out and grabbed his free hand. She squeezed so tight it was almost painful. "Marriages take love. Any work involved is a labor of that love. Don't you ever think anything can substitute for the love part. I know. I tried."

Garth was not encouraged as he leaned his hip against the counter and crossed his feet. "But you lost the man you—" He shook his head refusing to call the blind loyalty his mother had shown toward his father love. "Why try?"

"I lost because all the *trying* in the world couldn't substitute for the fact that he didn't love me. He never had."

Garth saw red. "So you forgave him by blaming yourself?"

"No, son," Frieda said, shaking her head now. "I forgave him because he asked me to. He was wrong, wrong, wrong in what he did. By going to that woman, he committed sin. He asked me to marry him when he knew he didn't love me. That was wrong, too. But I did something wrong, as well. I said yes, knowing full well that he didn't love me the way I loved him."

Frieda shook her head again and took a sip of Garth's milk. "I was going to work at that marriage and make him love me. It doesn't work. We proved that.''

Had he ever understood what his family had been about? ''Why did he ask? Why did you say yes?'' Suddenly, Garth needed to know. Needed to see that there was no correlation between his and Amanda's forced wedding—between what he felt for Amanda and what his parents had or hadn't shared.

''He wanted his grandfather's business, but he knew it wouldn't be handed over to him until he had a wife. I was always there in the background, adoring him. Ever since we met in high school, I loved him. And then, suddenly he saw me. He thought I would be the perfect wife. In his defense, I think he tried to love me but… Well, anyway, I forgave him. I had to.'' When he would have protested, Frieda put her hand up halting his objection. ''I had no choice. Don't you understand that, yet? It was for myself. I needed to let go of the hate. And really, when you think about it, Almighty God forgives anyone for anything they've done as long as they ask it in the name of His Son. How could I refuse? His Son let himself be nailed to a cross and took all our sins on His shoulders and He forgives us even though we were the cause. It would be pretty small of me not to do the same. Wouldn't it?''

Garth, now haunted by more than his need for Amanda, got very little sleep that night. Exhausted, his eyes drifted shut at last. Words and names swirled in his mind, disturbing even that respite.

Forgiveness.

Jesus.
Father.
Love.
Amanda.

Chapter Twelve

"Dad? Could I talk to you?" Jason asked.

Garth looked up from the lawn mower that refused to start. He'd been puttering around with the thing for an hour and still hadn't a clue what was wrong with it. Jason was a welcome interruption. He sat on the cement floor of the garage and gestured for Jason to join him. "What's on your mind, kiddo?"

Jason settled on the cement floor facing Garth and leaned back on his elbows, his feet crossed at the ankles. A mirror of Garth's own position. "What's my name?" Jason asked.

"Jason," Garth answered automatically, momentarily confused. Then he understood. "Well, legally it's Jesse Powers."

"But I don't want to be Jesse Powers. I don't want to hurt Mom's feelings, either, but I think I'm Jason Jorgensen. And so do all my friends at school. My teachers, too."

"Oh, I see," Garth said. He did see but he let Jason explain.

"I'm weird enough to all of them already. When I go back to school, I'm going to have to explain it *and* my leukemia again. And now Mom is Mrs. Jorgensen, too. Right? When you guys sign my stuff, we'll have different names. It's like I'm not part of the family. Who am I, Dad?"

Garth sat up, crossed his legs Indian style and scooped Jason into his lap. "You're our son. Legally you aren't my son. You're my stepson but you know that doesn't matter, don't you? I couldn't be any more your father if I'd been there when you were born."

"But I don't want you to be my stepfather. I know my real father was a hero but I want to be Jason Jorgensen again. Teddy Connors was a foster son first. He used to be Teddy Upsall. Then the Connorses adopted him and now he's Teddy Connors. Can't you adopt me? I want you for my father. My real father's dead and can't be my father anyway."

Jason seemed to get more and more worked up as they talked. Garth knew that if the boy was worrying about this too much it could undermine his recovery. But then, talking about this to Amanda wasn't going to be easy, either. He'd have to approach her in just the right way after quite a bit of thought. And unfortunately, back to school time was approaching. "I'll tell you what? I'll see what I can do. You put this out of your head, okay. Mom and I will work something out. I'll talk to her about it and we'll let you know when it's all fixed. Okay?"

Jason jumped up and gave Garth a tight hug

around his neck. "Thanks, Dad! It's great how I can always talk to you. So, what's wrong with the mower?"

Amanda waved goodbye to Garth at the back door and watched him drive off. She stood there until the car disappeared from sight and, some minutes later, realized she was still staring after him like a moonstruck idiot. Get a grip, Amanda. The man barely knows you're alive, she told herself. He hardly spoke a word to her anymore. She refused to dwell on the lacks in her marriage as long as she still had one.

She grabbed her tape measure, her notebook and pencil and headed for Garth's upstairs study. Frieda had explained that his office was on the second floor because Karen hadn't wanted her "creation" downstairs marred by Garth's old comfortable furnishings. There was a small room on the first floor she hoped to fix up as a surprise for Garth and furnish with his own familiar things. She walked in and looked around with a critical eye.

There was nothing wrong with the burgundy leather furniture. In fact, it was perfect for a man's study. The bookshelves were well made and had lovely detail work. The tables were another thing altogether. They had to go.

The styling of the desk was perfect but she wasn't sure if it needed refinishing. It was so covered with papers that Amanda couldn't really see the top. As she moved some flight plans he'd been working on to the side, she came across a letter from the lawyer who'd handled the prenuptial agreements for them.

"A hearing in the case of the adoption of Jesse

Powers is set for 10:00 a.m. on August 19 before Master Fletcher.'' The sentence glared up from the page at her. *Adoption*. The word telegraphed itself painfully into Amanda's brain. Garth had started proceedings to adopt Jason.

Wouldn't that negate their previous agreement? That agreement he'd stated that he had no rights to Jason but that she was granting visitation rights. If he adopted Jason, that would give him the legal right to vie for custody in the event of a divorce. An event Garth had promised would happen.

All Amanda's old fears resurfaced. *Had* he married her to strengthen his claim to Jason as she'd originally thought? Had he just been trying to lull her into a false sense of security by not mentioning this adoption to her? She battled back the tears that flooded her eyes until she reached her room.

The constant uncertainty about her relationship with Garth had finally taken its toll. An overwhelming sense of fear and doom settled over her soul. Burying her face in her pillow, Amanda gave free rein to her tears.

When they were spent, anger began to replace the pain. She rolled to her feet and stalked to the phone. Garth, however, was already in the air. As she dropped the phone in the cradle, Amanda realized she had just almost done the exact thing to Garth that he had done to her over the medical expense refund.

Seconds later, Amanda found herself deep in prayer about her marriage and her unrequited love for her husband. Why was she married to a man who couldn't love her?

Because you didn't ask Him, a voice in her soul

whispered. *You just went ahead and married Garth. You didn't give Him a chance to solve the problem. Now you live in fear and suffer the pain of being unsure of your husband.*

Amanda stayed in her room all day, feigning a splitting headache. Between bouts of tears, she prayed, asking forgiveness for not asking the Lord's direction about marrying Garth and for the wisdom to approach him in the right way about what she'd seen. She had to learn his true motives, yet not cause a rift between them if those motives were pure ones. She found no answer as to what she would do if they weren't. About Jason or her broken heart.

Garth tossed his jacket on the chair in his study and looked around. He noticed the notebook lying on the desk that Amanda used to record all the information on her decorating. Next to it was a tape measure. He picked up the book and found the page she'd labeled for his study still empty. She hadn't written anything on the page. Her headache must have come upon her just after he'd left for the office.

Worried, he went to her room and tapped lightly on the door so he wouldn't wake her if she was deeply asleep. When no answer came, Garth decided to just peek in to see if she was all right. But Amanda wasn't sleeping. She was sitting in a chair on the far side of the room. Even in the gloomy light he could see that she look terrible.

"Amanda?" he called. "Didn't you hear me knock?"

She looked up and nodded.

Alarmed by her puffy, red-rimmed eyes, he

walked in and toward her. "What's wrong? You look as if you lost your last friend?"

"Leave me alone. Please. I'm fine. I just need time to sort out a few things."

Garth frowned. Sort out? What could she possibly need to sort out? He started to back out of the room but the sadness in her tone stopped him. If there was something he'd done to put that look of utter desolation on her face, he had to know. How could he make sure she was happy if he didn't know what made her *un*happy? "Maybe talking to someone would help. You know, put a fresh perspective on whatever it is you're wrestling with."

"Actually, your perspective is all I guess I need. When I went to check your desk to see if the top needed refinishing, I saw a letter from your lawyer scheduling a hearing about your adoption of Jason. What adoption? We never discussed it. And why do you want to adopt him?"

Garth sighed. This is what he got for not being up front about all this. The problem was that he hadn't been able to decide how to approach her. He'd made up his mind to say something soon. Definitely in the next few days before he had to go out of town. "I was going to talk to you about this soon. It isn't something I'd even thought about but I should have. *We* should have."

"We already made provisions for you to have visitation rights…ah…later…ah…after we—"

"But we're married now," Garth stressed, sick of thinking about that agreement. "And Jason's upset *now*."

"Jason's upset? About what? He never told me he was worried about anything."

"Confused is more like it," Garth explained, calmer now that he was able to focus on his son. He sat down on the bed opposite her chair so he could see her expression better. "He doesn't know what to call himself when he goes back to school."

Now confusion clouded Amanda's eyes. "Call himself? We decided months ago he was Jason to all of us."

"But legally he's Jesse Powers. He wants to be Jason Jorgensen the way he always has been. He's afraid the other kids will single him out even more if he comes back with a new name. If you'd looked further, you'd have seen a form to change his first name as well."

Amanda didn't seem too angry when she asked, "Why didn't anyone discuss this with me? And if you're going to change his name for him why must you adopt him?"

"The form would only change his first name. He asked me to adopt him, Amanda, and that would change his last name. I just didn't know how to ask you. But time was important since Jason was so upset about school and the confusion his new name would cause. He also said that since he was the only one in the house whose name was Powers that he didn't feel like part of the family. I figured that at least if the paperwork got started the school would object less to his keeping his name the same since legally it would be that way soon anyway.

"I hope you'll forgive me for not talking to you about this sooner. I really did intend to. I just kept putting it off. I got the ball rolling, figuring I'd come up with a way to bring this up without upsetting you. I'm sorry you were hurt, especially since that's what I was trying to avoid. If you object, I'll try to explain to Jason that you want him to keep his father's last name.''

Amanda's lower lip quivered and she launched herself into his arms. "I don't care. You're his father. I forgot all about his name. It's okay. It's really okay.'' Garth held on to her tightly when she started to cry in earnest. Eventually, she quieted and he realized she was asleep. Careful not to wake her he tucked her in and sat down in the chair. What had he done or said that made her cry if she was truly okay about the adoption? One thing was certain, Amanda was insecure in her position in his life and it had made her unhappy. Maybe it was time he began to show her how he felt about her.

"Is it comfortable?"

Garth gave the recliner he'd just tested a wistful look. "But you said you wanted to stick to authentic furnishings.''

Amanda blew her bangs off her forehead. And this man teased her for not understanding how airplanes fly! "Garth, the kitchen-family room addition is completely separate from the historical section of the house. It has French doors to a deck for heaven's sake. They did not have decks during the Revolutionary War.''

"Or refrigerators or dishwashers," Garth added, catching on, she hoped.

"Exactly. We'll just decorate that part of the

house and, of course, the bathrooms with a colonial flavor. That's what I did in the kitchen.''

Garth seemed to consider this. "So, I can have the recliner but not that entertainment center I liked?" He grinned and she knew he planned to tease her about something. She'd seen that look on his handsome face too often not to recognize it. "Amanda, this may come as a shock to you," he continued setting her up she was sure, "but, there weren't any electronics around then, either.''

"Very funny. Do you understand why we can't buy that entertainment center?''

He shook his head. "Not really. It was oak. They used oak for furniture back then.''

"Arrgghh! The entertainment center you liked was too modern looking. Think of the hours someone would have needed to spend planing and sanding all those rounded edges." She took his hand and dragged him over to the sofa they'd already decided on. She flipped through the swatches of available fabrics. "See this fabric? We cover that chair in this fabric and it gives it the right flavor just the way it does for this traditional sofa.''

"But what do we do about the TV, stereo and VCR?''

Amanda smiled, seeing her own opportunity to tease him. "Well, we could upholster them." At his look of horror she laughed. "But I have a better idea. I found something. It's an antique armoire. I thought if you like it, we could have Mr. O'Brien put shelving in it.''

"That way we hide all the electronics.''

"By George, I think he's got it!" Amanda exclaimed.

Garth chuckled and leaned down to kiss her in full view of the other store patrons. It was a lingering kiss—an arms-wrapped-around-her kiss—and it had a powerful effect on Amanda's emotions and senses.

"Let's go look at the bedroom furniture next," he said after lifting his lips from hers. The tone in his voice betrayed the effect the kiss had on him as well.

Dazed, Amanda let him take her hand and lead her to the salesman. Garth confused her more and more each day. What did he want from her? If he wanted what she thought he did when he kissed her like that, then why did he hold himself back? She had sent him every kind of signal she could think of to let him know that his attentions were welcomed but he'd always frowned and backed off. Way off.

At least until yesterday, she realized. He'd been away for a week. Did absence really make the heart grow fonder? she wondered. Amanda didn't think so. Their lack of contact while their work schedules kept them apart had done just the opposite. Was this sudden change she saw only gratitude for her work on the kitchen? Yesterday he had kissed her and had remained sweetly affectionate all afternoon and evening. But they'd still gone to separate rooms at day's end.

She looked up at him as he chatted with the salesman. He glanced at her, his eyes still warm as he smiled and gave her hand, the one he hadn't let go of, a squeeze. He sure hadn't backed away this time. *Please, Lord, don't let this be just gratitude.*

* * *

Two more weeks went by. Two weeks of warm, firm hugs. Two weeks of spicy, spontaneous kisses and hand holding. Two weeks of growing affection and attraction. The violets arrived just as Amanda put the final touches on the newly finished master suite. Frieda brought them to her and gave her a sly smile as she left.

The note read: "Violets to match your eyes. Have dinner with me. Just me. Pick you up in the family room at seven. A real date. G."

Amanda looked around the room and smiled. One mystery solved. At least she hoped so. Garth had gone along with any suggestion she'd made while they worked together to plan the house. Except one. The violets also matched the bedroom wallpaper Garth had stubbornly insisted upon. Amanda sniffed the nosegay in her hand. Not much aroma but so very sweet, nonetheless.

"You look beautiful," Garth said as he stood when Amanda came into the family room.

"Wow, Mom! Be careful not to spill anything on that dress. It's real fancy!" Jason added from his place on the floor. "And you know how messy spaghetti is."

Amanda glanced down at her royal blue dress. She'd bought it weeks ago but had never worn it, embarrassed by its soft, flowing, romantic style in the face of her platonic relationship with her husband. She tilted her head and considered Garth for a long moment. "Thank you. Both," she added with a smile for the two men in her life.

Garth swallowed with difficulty as he walked toward Amanda.

She looked up at him, her violet eyes sparkling and said, "You look very handsome, yourself."

And Garth breathed a mental sigh of relief. It was the first time she'd seen him in a suit and tie since the wedding. He wasn't really a suit-and-tie kind of guy. He'd worn uniforms for so many years that he was always unsure what tie went with what. He was also more nervous tonight than he had been the night of his first date, so it was good knowing he hadn't made a fashion faux pas with a navy suit, navy-and-white striped shirt and a paisley tie.

"I still don't see why I can't come," Jason grumbled. "I'm always good in restaurants. You both always say so. And I'd try to be neat and I wouldn't even ask for dessert."

"Not tonight, Jase," Garth said, never taking his eyes off Amanda. "Tonight's just for grown-ups." He leaned down and kissed her without thinking.

"Oh, yuck. Are you two going to start getting mushy like Todd's parents? I told him I didn't have to put up with this!"

Amanda giggled in the back of her throat and Garth lifted his head to glance at his son. He couldn't help but grin at the horrified expression on Jason's face. He treasured this kid more than life itself, but Jason was murder on a romantic moment.

"And that attitude, young man, is precisely why tonight is for grown-ups only. Now, give us a kiss good-night and we'll see you in the morning."

After they got in the car and Garth started down the drive Amanda glanced back at the figure waving furiously from the living room window. "He was really disappointed not to be coming with us. Do you suppose we—"

"No. We shouldn't." Garth didn't slow the car a bit. "All parents leave their children with sitters. Mom isn't even that. She's part of the family. He didn't care a bit about our plans until he found out that we were going to the Casa Roma. The kid's not part Italian is he?"

"Nope, just French," Amanda said, then laughed. "All Cajun French except for maybe an Indian maiden way back."

Garth shook his head and pulled to a stop at a red light. "Weird. I look enough like Jess Powers to be his double but we don't even have nationality in common."

She looked at him, suddenly serious. "You have nothing at all in common with Jess except your looks," she said quietly.

Garth's heart suddenly thundered in his chest. He stared at Amanda, her face illuminated by a nearby streetlight. He really thought he saw love in her eyes. He wanted to trust that love existed all of a sudden. That love didn't hurt. "That's the nicest thing you've ever said to me. I know he hurt you, Mandy. I want to make you happy. I want that more than my next breath. I—"

The blare of a horn made them both jump.

"The light's green," Amanda said, having glanced forward when he looked behind to see why the guy behind had leaned on his horn.

Muttering about lousy timing, Garth drove through the intersection and on to the exclusive Casa Roma.

Reservations being what they were at the posh new Main Line restaurant, they were seated immediately at a table screened off by lattice and greenery. Garth had stopped by earlier in the week and had asked for this specific table. He'd left nothing to chance about this entire night. He put his hand in his pocket, anxiously feeling for the small, velvet jeweler's case. She had to say yes. If she didn't, he was afraid he'd disgrace himself and cry like a baby, which was another reason he'd wanted so private a setting.

"Garth, this is lovely. I'd heard about this place but never imagined it could be this perfect," Amanda said. "Thank you for bringing me here."

"No. Thank you."

Amanda's smile faltered. "Thank…me?"

Garth didn't know what he'd said wrong but she'd looked stricken for a few seconds before stiffening her spine and trying to achieve the same smile once again. This one was a poor imitation.

He took her hand and kissed her knuckles. Her hands weren't as soft as they'd once been, a testament to all her work. Work? "Mandy, not thank you for all you've done at the house. Although we all appreciate what you've done. To be honest, the inside of the place always made me feel like a fish out of water, but that's not what tonight's about. I meant thank you for coming into my life and making what I thought was a full life so much better.

"I know, I'm lousy at this," he groaned. "It still sounds like…gratitude, doesn't it?"

She nodded, but a little smile played at the corners of her mouth.

"It's not. I…" The words *I love you* seemed forever buried so deep within himself that he couldn't find them for anyone, even Jason. He reached for them but came up with, "I don't want to lose you."

"I'm not going anywhere," she assured him.

But Garth was far from assured. And he wanted—no needed—her assurance that she would always be there, so this time he reached for the diamond wedding band he'd had made. It would replace the one that had been his grandmother's—the one given as part of that unholy bargain they'd made to keep Jason's health on an even footing. The one that meant a possible end to the first real happiness he'd ever known.

"Promise me," he said and handed her the box. "Marry me. Be my wife. Forever. For real, Mandy. Not just Jason's mother but my wife. Lie in my arms at night and smile at me in the mornings. Be there to make coming home after work special. Look at me when Jason's friends leave after a weekend and smile because we're tired and we're still together."

Amanda bit her lip against a rush of tears. This was so much more than she'd thought possible the first time marriage between them came up. And so much less than she'd hoped for because now that she loved him so deeply, she'd hoped for his love in return. But if not love, what was it in his eyes? It didn't matter, she told herself stoically. This was enough. It had to be.

"Garth, I already did promise. You would have needed to tell me to go because I will never leave you."

His eyes narrowed. "Chris said that but we haven't slept—"

"That's not the point. I made you a promise before God in that chapel. I always intended to keep it. No matter what. Even if you asked for the divorce, I would have been your wife in my heart on the day I died."

"So, you'll stay because of your vows," he said, his jaw tight.

Amanda looked down at the box he'd pressed into her hand. She'd mentioned God and now she could feel his anger building a wall between them. Needing a distraction, she opened the box. She didn't even try to stifle her gasp of delight. Nestled on a bed of white satin was a diamond wedding band, each small setting a copy of the one on her engagement ring. She looked up and saw pain in his eyes instead of anger.

Putting the ring on to the first knuckle, Amanda whispered, "In the beginning that was true. But that isn't the reason anymore." She extended her left hand and he took her hand but lowered his eyes, hiding his feelings. Amanda pressed on anyway. It did no good for her to hold back words that had never hurt her the way they had Garth. Maybe if he heard them enough he'd believe them. "I'll stay because of you. Because of the man you are. Because of the husband I know you can be. I'll stay because I don't know if I could leave you now even if you asked me to. I need to be with you, Garth. You're already my husband—in my heart as well as on paper. I love you."

Garth didn't say anything. She told herself it didn't matter. He just pushed the ring gently the rest of the way onto her finger to nestle it next to the other two he'd already given her. He looked up then, longing and frustration roiling in his eyes. It was as if he wanted to say he loved her, too, but couldn't get the words out. She knew instinctively that when he finally said, ''I need to hold you,'' it was far less than he wanted to say but true nonetheless. He stood without letting go of her hand. ''Dance with me.''

Amanda smiled as a quartet began to play somewhere in the room. ''My, you did have tonight planned. Music on cue. Imagine that.''

Garth chuckled and pulled her to her feet, gesturing behind her. ''They'd just picked up their instruments. My timing doesn't seem to be bad tonight after all.''

When they reached the dance floor, Garth tugged her close and Amanda went willingly, closing her eyes and resting her cheek on his shoulder. It felt so good to be in his strong arms, knowing he was hers. Knowing that there wouldn't be a divorce. If she didn't have his love yet, she had hope that someday she would. There was all the time in the world.

They danced several numbers in a row when Garth whispered. ''I need to hold you.''

She looked up into his molten gaze. ''You already are.''

He shook his head. ''Not like this. I need more, Mandy. I need you. Tonight. Every night.''

''Me too,'' she said, her throat tight with emotion. ''But Jason's still up. We'd have to explain why we're home so early.''

Garth grimaced then sighed. ''Maybe we'd better eat something. Dance a little more. Something—anything to kill time. He'll be up for at least two more hours." He kissed the knuckle where his rings rested. "I know it sounds selfish but I want this to be just about us."

And it was. Just about them. For the rest of the night and into the early morning hours. It was about them and a union the Lord had blessed months earlier.

Amanda's prayers were answered.

She was Garth's wife.

Amanda woke to the sound of Jason's running feet and her name bouncing off the wall of the hall.

"Mom!" Door open. Door slam. "Mom!" Feet pounding to the top of the stairs. "Grandmom! I can't find Mom!"

"So much for discreetly taking my mother aside and explaining the change in...our uh..."

She giggled at his hesitancy. "How about we just say our relationship?"

Garth cleared his throat. "Good word," he said.

Amanda rolled over. "You're blushing!"

"Amanda, I do not—"

"Dad, I can't find Mom!" Jason called as he threw open the door and burst into the room with a full head of steam. His eyes widened. "Dad, how come your face is so red? Oh, Mom, there you are." He ran and dove between them on the bed. "You promised me pancakes for breakfast. It's past ten! Grandmom said not to keep looking for you but, Mom! She's threatening to make them herself. You've got to get up!"

"Threatening? Don't you mean offering," Amanda reproved.

Jason shook his head fiercely.

"Burned on one side—raw on the other," Garth muttered. "In defense of our son, Mandy, he means threatened."

"Okay, go tell Grandmom I'm on my way down."

"Hold on right there, son. We need a new rule here."

Jason wrinkled his nose. "Another rule?"

"Yes. Another rule. An important one. Now that this room's been redone, your mother is going to share it with me. You are never to barge in here like that again."

"Why?" Jason asked. "I always have."

Garth searched for the right words. Did this parenting thing never get any easier? "I wasn't always married, son. You're old enough to understand that your mother needs her privacy. Like Grandmom."

"Why?"

Amanda chuckled.

"Let me put it to you this way," Garth said with a glance at Amanda. "Would you like Debbie Culver walking in on you when you're in the bathtub?"

Jason blushed. "No! Oh! I get it! Okay, I'll knock."

"*And* wait for permission to come in. Got it?"

"Wait for permission," Jason said and nodded. "Got it."

"Good," Garth replied, then gave Jason a light, playful smack on his backside. "Now beat it so we can get dressed." Jason bounded off the bed and sailed out the door. "And get dressed yourself," Garth called after the retreating figure who'd forgotten to close the door behind him.

* * *

An hour later Jason ran out the back door with Buster tripping over his own paws as he followed. They watched from the window over the sink as Jason attempted to teach the puppy the rudiments of fetching. Amanda sighed wistfully and nestled her head on Garth's shoulder, her arms wrapped around his waist. He smiled and dropped his cheek on to her soft hair, hugging her back.

"He looks better and better each day," she said. "It's great having him here with me but I can't wait till he can go to school like a regular kid."

"But for now he is here. Almost all the time. And this isn't going to work."

"What's not going to work?" she asked, her voice suddenly wobbly and tinged with fear.

Garth cringed. *Open mouth—insert foot, Jorgensen.* He tipped her chin up and kissed her forehead. "I meant what I said about us last night and nothing's going to change that. What I meant was that just now us being here with Jase and Mom isn't good. We need time alone, Mandy. Just you and me. We need that honeymoon we never had and now's the perfect time."

"Go away? But what about Jason?"

He tipped her chin up farther so he could see her beautiful eyes. "Jason'll be fine. You said it yourself. He gets better and better each day. He's cured. I can feel it." He smiled at the thought.

"But—"

"My mother's here. Chris can stay here while we're gone to help out in the evenings. It isn't as if that isn't a familiar routine for him and it doesn't have to be for long. Just a few days."

"But the house and—"

"The house will be here when we get back and you can decorate to your little heart's content."

"What about Liberty Express?"

"It's been two years since I took a real vacation. The other pilots will be thrilled to take my hours. I've done it for them enough times."

"But you always say it isn't good business to have a plane sit idle. That's why you hired that temporary extra guy when Jason was so sick."

"It won't be idle. We'll be using it."

Amanda swallowed with obvious difficulty. "Using it?" she squeaked.

Garth chuckled. "If I didn't know better, Mrs. Jorgensen, I'd say you didn't trust my flying."

"Oh, no. It's just that the plane you brought me here in was so small. And bumpy. And noisy."

"And safe and convenient. No schedule to keep but our own. No annoying airport security to get past. No lines. No flights delayed for a dozen stupid reasons."

Amanda raised her eyebrows. "My, you do hate to fly commercial, don't you?" she teased.

"I wanted it to be just us but if my plane really scares you we'll fly commercial."

"No," she laughed. "Alone's just too tempting to resist. Besides, I trust you. Jason assures me you're the best pilot in the whole wide world. Where would we go?"

"I was thinking sort of a short tour. Maybe start out with Niagara Falls for a couple of days. Then a friend of mine has a resort in the Catskills. Riding, swimming, tennis. That sort of thing. It's on Hunter Mountain. Real pretty country. Come on, Mandy. It wouldn't even be for a full week. We have to be back for the hearing on the nineteenth. How about it?''

''It sounds wonderful. When would we leave?''

''It'll take a couple of days to arrange everything at work and make reservations. I'd need to file a flight plan, too. Then we'll be all set.''

Amanda threw her arms around Garth's neck and pulled his head down for a kiss. He closed his eyes willing the rest of the world away.

''Oh, excuse me,'' his mother said as she quickly backed out of the room.

Garth groaned and opened his eyes. Amanda winked and chuckled. ''Maybe you could make those arrangements in one day?''

Chapter Thirteen

Amanda glanced at her suitcase where it rested by the door. She was all packed and ready for their honeymoon trip. And so excited she felt like a kid on her way to Disney World instead of a thirty-something woman on her way to Niagara Falls.

They'd leave after lunch but first there was church.

Normally Amanda looked forward to those couple of hours on Sunday morning. They rejuvenated her and washed away the hassles of the week. But today she felt as if she were leaving a part of herself behind. Garth.

After checking her hair in the mirror one last time, Amanda turned to follow Frieda and Jason to the car. But as she passed the stairs she stopped. Once again her thoughts turned to Garth. How did he while away the time when the rest of them were at church? What was he doing and what was he thinking right now? From experience, she knew he wasn't getting ready to go with them.

As usual he'd made himself scarce after breakfast,

avoiding the inevitable questions from Jason and invitations from her and his mother. Fighting the melancholy feeling that had come over her, Amanda forced herself to move forward. She needed this even if Garth refused to realize that he did, too.

Garth pushed aside the drop cloth that hung over the window in the empty front bedroom. He watched, his fist clenched, as Amanda backed down the driveway. The car hesitated for a long moment then slowly drove away.

He threw the cloth back into place. Why couldn't she have given up church to be with him for just this week? This was supposed to be the day they started their honeymoon. Why couldn't she have wanted to be with him more than her God?

He guessed that was what he'd always wanted. Someone who put him before everything and everyone else. Someone who would count on him for everything. But she couldn't count on him for everything the way she counted on God. He remembered that bleak look in her eyes when he excused himself from the breakfast table—a tacit refusal to accompany her to church. Garth wanted more than anything to make Amanda happy and more often than not he made her miserable.

He couldn't protect her or Jason the way God could, either. Jason had gotten sick while under Garth's protection. Sure, God hadn't protected him then, either, but Amanda had said God would use all that pain and anguish for good. She'd said that He had a plan. And He obviously had since it really was Jason's illness that had brought Amanda to them.

Was she right? Could it all be that simple? He

sighed, remembering a time when he'd believed it was.

Now with the future looming on the horizon, he had to wonder about a lot of things. Like what made him think he'd be able to do any better in the future than he had in the past? Garth raked his unsteady hand through his hair. The answer scared the life out of him. He just didn't see how he could go it alone anymore.

If only Amanda were there to tell him that he'd do fine. Anger flared in his heart once again. He needed her! Why couldn't she have stayed home?

What stopped you from going with her? Pride? Because you said you didn't need her fairy tales and crutches? You wanted to go it alone. Why start whining about how hard it is now?

"Because it doesn't have to be this way!" Garth shouted at the voice that had been whispering to him from a distant corner of his mind for years. His voice echoed in the empty room—in the deserted house. And this time he listened.

It didn't have to be this way. It didn't!

He could go back to the one source of strength that had never failed him. Things might not have been easy when he was young but he'd always had his faith to bolster him even in the roughest of times. Even when he'd learned his father's plans to get rid of his wife and take a new one.

Garth slid down the wall to the floor, momentarily shocked. But then he thought back to the night he'd chucked it all and turned his back on his faith and his Lord. It *hadn't* happened when he'd stood in the hall outside his father's study. Somehow through the years he'd convinced himself and everyone else that it had been.

But it hadn't.

No, it had been after the meeting with the pastor when he'd told him what he'd learned. He hadn't gone to the man because he wanted to protect his church from scandal and disgrace. He'd gone there with a spirit of revenge in his heart against his father. His father had betrayed them all and had to pay with the one and only thing that had ever mattered to him. He had to lose his church.

After he'd told his tale, Garth had felt ashamed. He'd rushed to judgment, and committed his own sin of seeking vengeance. Then anger had taken hold of his young heart. He had all the guilt and his father expressed nothing but anger at him for his betrayal. And then Garth's anger had exploded. He'd turned his back on God the same way his father had turned his back on his family.

And that was why he was still angry. His father had sought forgiveness and been granted it. Garth had never admitted that he'd been wrong. In deed and in motivation. He should have let his parents deal with their own marital problems. But he hadn't and for all that he'd never sought forgiveness and so he still felt guilty—and angry. In fact, Garth realized with yet another pang of guilt, in going to the pastor and shutting his father out, he had been guilty of the same sort of pride and perfectionism his father had always shown toward him.

Garth dropped his head back against the wall and closed his eyes.

Amanda's drive to the small stone church that sat nestled in a wooded area took only a few minutes but today she felt as if she'd driven miles. She felt so far away from Garth. Probably because they'd scarcely been out of each other's sight since he had taken her to Casa Roma the other night. If only he'd come with them today, she thought, as she slid into the pew after chatting with several of the other parishioners.

Lost in thought and prayer, Amanda automatically opened her mouth to sing along with the choir when the music started. But the joyful noise she'd intended to sing unto the Lord turned into a gasp when a beautiful, clear, tenor voice next to her sang the opening words of "Amazing Grace."

Though Amanda had never heard Garth sing, she knew instantly that it was his voice raised in praise. She pivoted and stared up at him. He stood in the aisle, singing from memory. Tears of joy clogged Amanda's throat and blurred his beautiful smile, but her ears still worked just fine and it was plain that Garth meant each word. How or why he was there, she didn't know.

But she rejoiced.

He leaned down and kissed her cheek and settled his arm around her when the pastor took his place at the podium and dismissed the children to their classes. Curiosity and overwhelming joy all but obliterated the message for her, though Garth seemed intent on the lesson. Finally the congregation rose as one to sing the final song of the service.

"How? What happened?" she asked as soon as the pastor disappeared up the aisle to greet his parishioners as they filed out.

Garth shrugged. "I felt left out. I missed you after

you drove away and I was angry that I was alone. I started to worry about you and Jase. I felt weak and afraid of the future. Afraid I'd fail you both. I needed to hear you telling me I was doing okay by you and Jason. I needed you and I was furious that you weren't there.''

"But you knew you were welcome, didn't you?" Amanda said, worried that she'd somehow failed him when he'd needed her.

"I knew. I was just plain stubborn. Then this morning I suddenly realized that it was me who'd stayed home. It was me who'd cut himself off from all this. The joy. The comfort. The forgiveness. A part of you. This part of you. And Him."

Amanda reached up to lay her palm on his cheek. "Oh, Garth, I'm so glad you finally understand."

Garth took her hand in his. "It may take a while to work it all out. I'm carrying a lot of baggage because of my father that I've never dealt with. But at least I can admit it now. I see it for what it is and I see that he was just a man. Imperfect. Flawed. Not an angel or a god. And his mistakes were his, not God's. Not mine."

"And now we can share everything," Amanda whispered.

"Even eternity," Frieda said and held out her arms to her son, tears rolling down her wrinkled cheeks. "Welcome home, son. Welcome home."

Five days later Amanda thought back to the scene in the church as she watched the trees fly by beneath them. She and Garth were returning from their honeymoon. Their wonderful honeymoon that had

shut out the view of the trees remembering how the
pastor had returned to where she and Garth stood and
presented him with a Bible. He'd been saving it, he'd
said. The man had known Garth's father, had been
with him at his death. Edward Jorgensen had sent his
son a message to be delivered when he was ready to
hear it. The pastor decided then was a good time.

Amanda still reserved judgment on that one.

She knew it had shaken Garth's fledgling faith but
only for a couple of seconds. Garth had done the
right thing in going to their pastor, his father had
said. There were no hard feelings. That was it. He
hadn't asked for forgiveness for all the pain he'd
caused. He hadn't said he was proud of Garth or his
accomplishments.

But Garth had nodded after a few heartbeats and
held her against his side, obviously feeling her reaction. "It's okay. It doesn't matter that he didn't
ask my forgiveness. It just matters that I'm forgiven," he'd whispered and she'd heard the amaze-
ment in his voice.

Amanda's first thought had been that she wanted
to hurt Garth's father posthumously until she saw
that it really didn't matter to Garth. But it made her
more aware than ever that sometimes being a Christian was a tough road to follow and that no one succeeded all the time. Especially not her.

And speaking of roads, she thought now, there
were none below them. Only millions of acres of
trees. "We're really in the wilderness, aren't we?"

"Yeah, this section of the Catskills is pretty
sparsely populated. In the winter, skiers flock up here
but at this time of the year, before the color really

"I meant that I haven't seen a road in an awfully long time."

Garth chuckled. "The roads are there. They're hidden by the trees. I could look for an interstate if it would improve the scenery for you."

"But if you had to land..."

"This King Air is Liberty's newest plane, Mandy. I had it gone over nose to tail by the best mechanic around before we took off. Relax."

"I am. Really," she lied. She knew that quake in her voice gave her away so she changed the subject a bit. "I still feel guilty that you took a plane this big out of service just because the Piper scared me when you flew us to Philadelphia. You should have just used that one."

"I wasn't having you trembling in your seat the whole trip, sweetheart. It wouldn't have been fair. This is supposed to be fun." Garth reached over and gave her hand a quick squeeze before returning it to the yoke. Where she wanted it anyway!

"Still, those twenty-five seats sitting empty back there make me feel guilty."

Garth flashed her a crooked grin. "It would have been worth it if the bigger plane had given you a bit more confidence in my flying."

"It isn't your flying ability that worries me. It's Newton and Murphy's laws that keep me on edge." Amanda forced a smile. She was only half joking but he didn't need to know that!

Garth raised an eyebrow. "Newton and Murphy?"

"Sure." Amanda shot him a wry smirk. "What goes up must come down? If anything can go wrong it will go wrong?"

ised. Then, after reaching to flip a switch on the control panel, he twisted to face her, leaning negligently on the arm of his seat. "So, what was your favorite part of Niagara Falls?"

Amanda's eyes strayed to the now guideless yoke. Garth reached out and took her chin. "Look at me. It's on autopilot. This is called changing the subject. Now, what was your favorite part?"

"How do you pick a favorite part of a dream come true?" she answered, unable to look away from his compelling gaze. "I guess Monday afternoon and the picnic in the state forest." For Amanda, having Garth whisper that he wanted her to have his baby almost made her most fervent dream come true. The only thing that could have made that moment more perfect would have been hearing the words "I love you" whispered as well. Someday, she told herself once again.

Someday.

He leaned forward and closed the gap between them, joining his lips to hers in a fleeting kiss. "Mine was the nights," he whispered from inches away. "Scenery and hiking and picnics could never compare to holding you in my arms."

Amanda didn't bother to correct his misconception. "I'll never forget the nights, either. Do you think one of those nights will give you your wish?"

"Wish?"

Amanda nodded. "The wish you made on the picnic."

She watched as the memory of his picnic wish surfaced. He grinned. "If not we'll just keep trying."

"Mmm-hmm," Amanda agreed, leaning back in

plan, thought I doubt it will be necessary. I have a feeling Jason's going to have a brother or sister in the spring," she said, opening her eyes, not wanting to miss his reaction.

Joy then tenderness stole over Garth's features. "Really?"

Amanda nodded.

"How can you know so soon?"

"I'm so tired I can hardly keep my eyes open and I've only been awake for what? Five or six hours? This is just the way I was within days of conceiving Jason."

"Wow," he said, his tone more reflective than excited. "Think Jason will be pleased?"

"I hope so," she said, unable to keep the wistfulness out of her voice.

"Miss him?" Garth asked.

Amanda turned her head and opened her eyes again. He looked rather jaunty in his flight jacket, Liberty Express baseball cap tipped back on his head and wearing those official-looking headphones. "Not as much as I'd have missed these last days with you. Thanks for insisting. We really did need this."

"Why don't you try to get some sleep?" Garth looked at Amanda, smiled and then winked. "You might be sleeping for two now."

After settling back and closing her eyes again, Amanda muttered, "You just want me unconscious so I'll stop twitching at every noise." Garth's chuckle was the last thing she heard before she drifted into sleep.

Amanda's nap ended with a crash the likes of

heart pounding. The plane dipped sharply then bounced back up—hard. Amanda felt as if her stomach were still in free fall. Her next confused perception was that night had fallen around them suddenly but there was too much ambient light for that. The plane was vibrating like a car being driven along railroad tracks. She could see Garth's hands gripping the yoke in what looked like a life-and-death struggle.

She looked at his face. The look of strain carved there was answer enough to her unasked question. It was a life-and-death struggle. Then Garth's gaze met hers.

"Don't fall apart on me, Mandy. I need your help." Once again the plane shook, buffeted by surging winds. "I can't take my hands off the yoke."

"What happened to that autopilot thing?"

"Not working—like a lot of the other systems. I need you to put your hand on one of the knobs on the control panel. Okay. Now, move it over two to your left."

The plane dropped altitude suddenly, leaving Amanda's stomach what felt like a hundred feet above them. Once again, Garth fought for and gained control of the rocking craft as thunder and lightning crashed around them.

"Did I do that? I swear I didn't touch anything."

"It was the wind. It's okay," he said as the plane evened out again. He glanced back at her hand. "That knob only sets the radio frequency. Turn it to 121.5. That'll put us on the emergency band. Good. Now move your hand down one and to your right. Turn that one to 7700. Right. That puts the tran-

zero in on us on their radar screen when I raise a tower. Say a prayer there's one not too far away. This bird's in sad shape.''

''That's so they can find us, right? Are we lost? Don't you know where we are?''

''With my instruments out I can't pinpoint our location exactly but I've got a good idea.'' He sounded so confident that she almost missed the slight inflection in his tone.

''Where are we?'' she asked, dreading what she guessed might be a vague answer.

Garth grimaced. ''Somewhere over the Poconos.''

Amanda sighed. ''What happened?''

''A thunderstorm came from nowhere. Nobody was reporting it. Lightning hit the starboard engine. Now sit back and get your head against the headrest. And Mandy, I meant what I said about praying. I don't want to lie to you. We're in real trouble here and I'm going to have to concentrate on flying.''

Then in a controlled voice Garth spoke into the headset he wore. ''Mayday. Mayday. This is LIB 7985. Anyone within range come in, please.''

He sat a bit straighter. ''Canadensis tower. This is LIB 7985. I'm experiencing what looks like a total electric failure after a lightning strike,'' he answered what must be a voice coming through his earphones.

''A Beech King Air.... It hit the starboard engine.... I've been losing oil pressure and fuel ever since.... It's still up and running rough. I can't be sure for how long.... One passenger. My wife. Have you picked up my transponder reading...? Roger. Changing course to those coordinates.''

Amanda released the death grip she had on the arm

"The electrical system's acting up. So's the engine that was hit."

"I heard. It sounds like a big problem."

"The electric is the real trouble. Not too much works right without it. Like the autopilot. But we got lucky. There's an airfield only about fifteen minutes to the southwest. We'll be landing there." Garth immediately made the course correction he needed to put them back on course. The plane banked. Not smoothly, but he did seem to get it to do what was necessary.

Amanda could feel perspiration bead on her scalp. Her fingers were already numb from the tight grip she kept on the arms of her seat. She marveled at how calm and competent he was. "Are we going to crash?" she asked, her voice nowhere near as steady as Garth's.

"Not if I can help it. I've got too much to live for and so do you. We just found each other and Jason needs us. And there's that baby you seem so sure we'll be having in the spring." He looked away and she could see the muscles of his jaw tighten as if he were fighting for control.

He glanced back at her, his eyes misty. "Amanda, I'm going to need more help. Do you remember asking me what that crank in the back of the plane is for?"

"You said it was the manual crank for the landing gear."

"Yeah. I need you to go back and turn it as far as you can. As hard as you can. Can you do that?"

"You also said you'd never used it."

Garth's grin was as easygoing as she knew he

could make it. "Well, there's a first time for everything, sweetheart."

Amanda twisted in her seat and stared backward down what she'd thought of as a short aisle earlier. Then the plane pitched to the side and lost altitude. She sat frozen. How was she going to get there? What if she wasn't strong enough to crank down the landing gear?

"I can't leave the controls, Mandy, and that gear won't come down automatically with the electric system off-line. Come on. You can do it. Undo your safety belt. Get down on the floor. I want you to crawl back. I don't want you falling and hurting yourself. This is about as steady as I can hold her."

Garth didn't add that injured or unconscious she'd be little help to them and he didn't relish landing with no chance that the gear was down. As it was, with no indicator lights to show that the gear had locked, they could only hope and pray that it did. "Remember, turn it as far and as hard as you can."

Three minutes went by in agonizing slowness for Garth as he took instructions from the tower and Amanda crawled to do her best with the crank. The control tower had called out emergency equipment but that didn't give him much confidence. This wasn't Philly International's tower he was linked up with. It was a small backwater airport. He was lucky they had radar. He'd flown in and out of there several times. Their tower was two stories tall and the emergency team consisted of gas station attendants, a café waitress and a cook who'd been a medic in the marines.

Once again, a sudden wind shear tossed them

a screech at the back of the plane nearly had him abandoning the controls. "Amanda!"

"I'm okay. A little bruised but I'll live," she called. "I think I got the gear down. The latch on the door to the rest room came loose and hit my head."

Garth didn't miss the irony in her voice when she said that she'd live. She *had* to live through this. Even if he didn't. "Then belt yourself in back there," he called.

"But I want to be with you," she shouted back.

"It's safer back there, sweetheart."

About a minute later, there was a shuffling next to him as Amanda wiggled back up into her seat from the floor. "But I want to be with you," she repeated. "Garth, if the landing gear is down, why didn't those three red lights turn green the way you showed me when we landed in New York?"

"Because the electrical system's out." Amanda held his gaze and somehow with just her eyes, she forced him to tell her the rest. "We can't know if it locked, Mandy."

"Until it does or doesn't collapse?" He nodded. "I'm scared, Garth. If we don't make it, what's going to happen to Jason?"

The starboard engine choked just then causing the plane to falter even more. Garth fought for control then feathered the engine. The plane dropped a bit more altitude but that was okay. He'd be taking her down soon anyway. For good or bad. This ride was almost over. He glanced at Amanda. Pale, frightened and thinking of Jason. She'd been cheated of so much.

*ing Jason grow. Don't cheat her of having our baby.
Give me the strength and wisdom to do this right.
Lock that landing gear.*

"Nothing bad's going to happen to Jason because
nothing's going to happen to us. God didn't bring us
together just to take us away from Jason. I've been
in tougher spots than this and lived to tell the tale."

But never with the woman you love—the mother
of your son—sitting next to you, he thought. He
looked at her long and hard, memorizing each feature
in case memories had to last an eternity.

The woman he loved.

*And are you ever going to get up the guts to tell
her how you feel? It's only a little word. And it'd
mean so much to her. Are you going to cheat her of
hearing you say it? One or both of you could die and
you'll never have said it. She'd never know,* he chas-
tised himself silently.

"Amanda, there's something I have to tell you before I take us in for a landing. It's not the best setting
or circumstance. I can't even hold your hand let
alone hold you in my arms the way I want to but I
think it had better be now, sweetheart. I—I love you.
I love you with all my heart. I'm sorry I never told
you how I felt before, but the word wouldn't come.
It was thrown back in my face so often as a kid that
I swore never to say it again. Then even when I
wanted to, I couldn't. I didn't mean to hurt you."

Amanda's smile was gentle as she blinked back
tears. "I was hurt, but it doesn't matter because I
love you. All that matters is that you do."

Garth's attention was snatched away just then. The
tower had a visual sighting on them and started giv-

blue lights of the runway came into sight for him as well. Garth braced the yoke with his knees and took a second to give Amanda's cold hand a squeeze. "Okay, sweetheart, here we go. Put your head down on your knees and lock your hands behind your head. Pray real hard, Mandy, I want a hug and kiss when this is all over."

Garth lined them up and started the rocky descent. *Hold us up, Lord. And set us down easy,* he prayed.

After all the fear and worry, Amanda nearly laughed at how perfect the landing went. When she felt the plane roll to a stop, she would have laughed. She really would have, but she was too busy shedding tears of joy in Garth's loving arms.

Epilogue

Garth ran through the hospital lobby and dove for the call button at the middle of the bank of elevators. He bumped into an older man who had approached from the other direction. "Sorry," Garth said, then turned to the controls and repeatedly stabbed it. "Come on. Come on."

"In sort of a hurry, son?"

"Yeah. My baby's having my wife! Three weeks early!" Garth exclaimed and stabbed the call button again. "Why isn't this elevator coming?"

"Don't say?" The old man chuckled, raising one of his thick gray eyebrows. "Sort of nervous, too. This your first?"

Garth shook his head. "Fourth. Well, third really. I wasn't around for the first. Sometimes I'm almost glad I wasn't. My wife's afraid of needles. Has them natural. It's awful. She needs me." He stabbed at the button again then again when it refused to stay lit.

"Ah, son. The elevator's here. You'll want to be getting on, won't you?"

Garth turned toward the old man's voice and rushed into the elevator, stabbing the number five on the control panel. "Bye and thanks," he shouted over his shoulder seconds later when the elevator doors slid open and he charged out. Jason was there to greet him.

"Mom's fine. So's the baby. But you better get in there," he said directing Garth toward Amanda's labor room at a fast clip. "Doc Hernandez was by a few minutes ago and said it won't be much longer."

"If you're here, who's with Ian and Patrick?" Garth asked.

"Grandmom, Aunt Chris and the terrors are in the waiting room. We've got everything under control. You go take care of Mom," his son ordered. "And give her my love."

Garth nodded and entered the room where their child would be born—three weeks early. Amanda looked toward him and smiled. It was one of her brave, I'm-in-pain-but-okay smiles. It didn't calm his pounding heart a bit. "I'm getting too old for this, lady," he quipped as he took her hand and smiled. No IV. She'd once again managed to convince the staff that an IV wasn't necessary. He lifted her hand and an eyebrow.

Amanda chuckled. "They really respond well to hysterics around here."

Garth leaned forward and kissed her forehead just as her hand tightened on his. "Jason sends his love. How far apart are the pains?"

"Right...on top...of one...another," she said through gritted teeth.

Garth looked around at the empty room and felt

the blood drain from his head. "Then where are your doctor and all the nurses?"

"Ah, the sound of a panicking father. Sweet music to my ears," Maria Hernandez, now Doctor Maria Hernandez, said. Garth glanced at the doorway as she rushed in, an entourage of begowned women hurrying in behind her. "I was just dressing for the occasion," she continued. "Glad you could make it. Sorry about the unscheduled arrival."

"Are you sure this isn't too early?"

"Babies arrive this early all the time. No sweat. So, Mom. Ready to push this one out into the world?"

Garth was exhausted. Which was ridiculous. It was Amanda who always had to do all the work. He grinned knowing he looked like an idiot. She'd outdone herself this time. Little Jessica was perfect. She didn't look a bit like Ian or Patrick, who both looked like their mother. She was the picture of Jason. Same thick dark hair. Same stubborn little chin. It had been almost like watching Jason being born. Except at the end when he'd seen that he finally had a daughter. Jessica.

Garth hoped Jess Powers was in heaven looking down. He hoped he understood why they had named their daughter after him. He hoped Jess understood why his son no longer carried his name and that he was proud of the tall, healthy boy he'd fathered.

Six years had passed with no recurrence of Jason's leukemia. He was considered cured by the medical community. Though God had somehow let Garth know that years ago, it was nice to have science confirm it.

He walked toward the waiting room but stopped when he heard Ian's five-year-old voice. "Tell us again how God used you to make us all a family."

"It was just like a fairy tale," Jason said, never tiring of telling the tale, "only it was real, like the miracles and stories in the Bible. A bad thing happened to Dad when he was young and he just didn't think he could love anybody ever again. And then he met this woman. She was sort of like one of those witches is in a fairy tale—a real bad lady—so it was good that Dad didn't love her. Anyway, she stole me from our mom when I was a baby. When the bad lady took me to Dad, he thought I was his son. He loved me right away but I'm not sure he knew it yet. Then the bad lady died."

"How she died?" two-and-a-half-year-old Patrick demanded.

"Ah..." Jason hesitated for a second. "She sort of fell into her own cauldron from what I hear. Well, anyway. Dad was still sad 'cause of the thing that had happened years before. He didn't find anybody else to love besides me until God finally stepped in. He let me get real sick and so Dad was real worried. And it was no fun for me, either, let me tell you."

"But it was worf it," Patrick said, obviously well versed with this, Jason's favorite story.

"It sure was worth it. Me getting sick let Dad find out who I really was. So, then he went on a search for Mom."

"Just like the prince in Cinderella," Ian added.

"Right. But instead of a shoe, Dad found a picture of Mom and me in the stuff the bad lady left behind. That led him to Mom. When he found her he put her in his plane and brought her to me. Then I could finally start to get better. While I got better, they fell in love and lived happily ever after.''

Garth stepped into the doorway of the waiting room, love overflowing his heart as he looked at his family and remembered the days when he and Jason had been alone. God truly had been good to him, Garth thought as he wiped away a tear. He'd sent Amanda to Garth. And though she had only married him for the sake of her child, Amanda had come to love him and had restored Garth's ability to believe in love. And best of all He had expanded their family so they both had more people to shower their love upon.

"Boys." Garth smiled. "The Lord sent you a sister."

* * * * *

Dear Reader,

I hope you've enjoyed *For the Sake of Her Child*. It was a true labor of love. Nothing can compare to the joy of doing what you love while serving the Lord. I hope I've done that by showing how He took two evil deeds, the murder of Amanda's husband and the kidnapping of her son, and made them work for good.

No matter how bad things are in our lives, as was certainly true for Amanda, Garth and little Jason during his illness, the Lord is in charge and can make all things work out.

Sometimes we pray and feel that He hasn't heard, but we need to remember the lesson Jason learned so young. Sometimes the answer is yes, but often it's wait. It may take years for Him to answer, but He *will* answer, just as it took years for Amanda to be reunited with Jason.

Remember also, sometimes His answer is no. We may lose a loved one, as Amanda did with her first husband, but He still may have good things in store for us. We just have to keep on believing and praying.

It took me a lot of years pounding away on first a typewriter and later a keyboard to get a manuscript accepted for publication. My nails wore grooves in my keyboard. But the Lord's answer was, Wait. And you know what? I believe that first sale probably felt a little sweeter for me than for some others who sold their first book.

So, whatever it is you're praying for, trust in the Lord. If achieving your heart's desire will be good for you, it'll happen. If it doesn't, then maybe He knows something you don't!

God Bless,

Kate Welsh

Take 3 inspirational love stories FREE!

PLUS get a FREE surprise gift!

Special Limited-time Offer

Mail to Steeple Hill Reader Service™
3010 Walden Avenue
P.O. Box 1867
Buffalo, N.Y. 14240-1867

YES! Please send me 3 free Love Inspired™ novels and my free surprise gift. Then send me 3 brand-new novels every month, which I will receive months before they appear in bookstores. Bill me at the low price of $3.19 each plus 25¢ delivery and applicable sales tax, if any*. That's the complete price and a saving of over 10% off the cover prices—quite a bargain! I understand that accepting the books and gift places me under no obligation ever to buy any books. I can always return a shipment and cancel at any time. Even if I never buy another book from Steeple Hill, the 3 free books and the surprise gift are mine to keep forever.

103 IEN CFAG

Name	(PLEASE PRINT)	
Address		Apt. No.
City	State	Zip

This offer is limited to one order per household and not valid to present Love Inspired™ subscribers. *Terms and prices are subject to change without notice. Sales tax applicable in New York.

ULI-198

©1997 Steeple Hill

The author of over fifteen inspirational
romances, Irene Brand brings
Love Inspired® readers a poignant and
heartfelt story.

HEIRESS

by

Irene
Brand

After discovering that she was the sole heiress to her
uncle's vast fortune, Allison Sayre embarked on an
amazing journey. She never imagined she would
uncover a shocking family secret. Or be drawn back
into the life of Benton Lockhart, a man whose
powerful spiritual convictions had once
inspired her....

Available at your favorite retail outlet from
Love Inspired.®

Steeple
Hill™

ILIHEIR

October 1998…

Love Inspired invites you to
experience the words of one of America's
best-loved writers…

Carole Gift Page

This talented author of over thirty-five
novels returns to Love Inspired with

RACHEL'S HOPE

Rachel Webber knew her unexpected pregnancy was a
blessing, but her joy was short-lived when her beloved
family began to unravel. Not only were she and her
husband, David, drifting further apart, but their
impressionable teenage son seemed to be suffering
most of all. Still, Rachel's enduring faith had always
illuminated her life. And now, more than ever, she had
to believe the good Lord would bring hope back into
all their lives....

Don't miss this emotional story about
the power of faith and love.

Available in October 1998 from

Available at your favorite retail outlet.